THE ROAD FROM OBLIVION

DRIVING FORCE: BOOK 1

GREG CHASE

BAYOU MOON PUBLISHING, LLC

ABOUT THIS BOOK

The Road from Oblivion Blurb

As the third-generation captain of the Beast—a century-old earth rover—Swash Jones has endured more than his share of loss. But that's the way it is for most people in post-apocalyptic North America. To keep his current crew alive, Swash will need to overcome the PTSD that haunts him.

Each member of the crew comes with particular challenges. Swash must be on constant watch for the trader who's after him for freeing his navigation expert—Whisper —from slavery. He also needs to guard the personal secret of Roach, his pilot, maintain a degree of separation from Stitch, the attractive medic who saved his life, and hang onto Blade, their hired-gun weapons master with a shady past.

Only by keeping his crew together can he maintain the Beast and hope to survive the wastelands, storms, and marauders of daily existence. When Whisper receives a message from her mother over a deactivated satellite, the crew members must combine their skills and test the limits of the Beast to meet the next challenge. Swash's team will soon prepare for a new mission—one that has the potential to save what's left of humanity.

1

---

*S*wash Jones hammered the earth rover's accelerator to the floor and cranked the wheel as a grenade exploded in front of the twenty-five-ton vehicle. "How fracking long is Scorch's reach? It's been over a year. He really needs to let this go." The flaming-earth sigils flying over the pursuing trucks left no doubt as to who was seeking the end of the Beast and its crew.

"I am sorry, Captain." In the navigator's chair, Whisper Payne struggled to keep her hands on the controls of the twin navigation drones flying half a mile ahead.

"For the hundredth time, it's not your fault. That butt tumor owed me a lot more than the cost of a freed slave. Focus on finding me a dry path out of here." The radiation overlay on the front view screen displayed the bay surrounding the Islands of Lost Angels in shades of Day-Glo green.

"On it," Whisper said. The three-dimensional

holographic map in front of the slip of a girl swung wildly as she shot the drones over foothills and beaches of radioactive debris.

The Beast's weapon's master, Blade, crashed into the hatch. His body filled the rounded opening. "I've got the plasma lances outfitted with cannon tips. Give me the word, and I'll blast those gas frackers to ash."

"Too hot." Swash smashed the Beast into a grove of dead trees so desiccated they splintered into kindling. Green radioactive termites spewed from the trunks, covering the Beast's view screen in putrid goo.

"Tell that to those petrol heads," Blade said. "I can smell their exhaust from here."

Blade was prone to exaggeration when itching for battle. The air intakes at the back of the rover decontaminated the Beast's air supply. They also filtered out and stored water and any potentially useful chemicals.

Swash leaned over the wheel as the airless rubber-and-metal front tires careened over a boulder. "We exhausted Stitch's supply of Iodine-X during that last boondoggle. I can't risk you standing out on the catwalk and suffering further exposure."

"How was I supposed to know that water was contaminated?" Blade asked.

Swash wasn't in the mood to deal with the big man's whining. "Head to the back hatch. The moment Stitch says we're in the clear, I'll turn you loose on those sand maggots." He nudged the headset with his jaw. "Roach, how're we coming with the go-juice?"

"Just adding the last gallon now. That'll leave two in the jump spider."

Swash itched to hit the hyper-power button, but with their limited supply of high-octane alcohol, he dared not waste a drop. "Stay with the engines. Our girl doesn't always respond well to being kicked in the ass."

"Just give me a heads-up, boss," Roach said.

"I've got a path, Captain." Whisper reached over to the view-screen controls and projected the map overlay. A snaking red line cut through the long-dead forest and tumbled boulders.

Sweat beaded on Swash's forehead. "You have to be kidding me. That's straight into marauder territory. We've spent the last three months *avoiding* those canyons."

Whisper turned away from the hologram to look Swash in the eye. "It's the best I can do, Captain."

Swash took a tree trunk right in the center of the view screen. Even the termites looked terrified as they squirmed away from the oncoming battle. "Stitch, I could really use the all clear right about now."

Back in the crew quarters, in her med closet, the med tech was working her scientific magic. "Almost there, Swash. Another mile should do it."

"We may not have another mile."

The oversized tires jumped a small ledge and landed on the rutted remains of a roadbed. Roads meant ambush, busted axles, and complete exposure, and this one was no exception. The moment the back tires hit the pavement a barrage of projectiles started peppering the Beast's roof.

"Send him out," Stitch said. "So long as we can scavenge

some Iodine-X in the next forty-eight hours, I can decontaminate whatever he breathes in."

"Thanks, Stitch." Swash swerved the giant rover into the path of a marauder truck that was trying to squeeze by.

"I'm already out the door," Blade yelled. His words were immediately followed by an arching blast of lightning that backlit the rover.

With a quick check of the rear-facing view screen, Swash saw nothing behind them but dust and falling boulders. He angled his jaw against the headset. "Blade, dial down that power. I don't need you draining the batteries before we're even halfway through the canyon."

"Whatever."

Another arching blast lit up the rock walls ahead, sending boulders crashing down and rolling over four incoming trucks. Swash hit the suspension lifts. What the rocks started, the rover finished, turning the trucks into metal pancakes.

"I could use a little better drone input," Swash yelled to Whisper.

"I'm recalling them now. One more gang of marauders around the next bend, then we'll be clear."

"Copy," Blade yelled over the intercom. "My rear blast seems to have plugged Scorch's army. I'm headed to the front mounts. Try not to bounce me off the catwalk."

"No promises," Swash grumbled without activating the headset.

"Shit," Whisper yelled. "Incoming fire drones. They've got me." The holographic zapped into nothingness, but the map on the view screen remained. "Goodbye, little hummingbirds."

The small navigation drones weren't exactly expendable, but Swash did still have six in reserve. "Okay, Roach. Time to lay in the go-juice. Everyone, strap in. I'm getting us the hell out of this tar trap."

Swash waited until Blade locked the plasma canyon into the bow port mount and hooked his harness to the railing. Then he lifted his foot from the pedal, reached down next to his knee, and shoved the go-juice booster lever forward. The screaming whirl of the turbos coming up to full pressure hurt his ears. Lights on the dash switched from red to green.

"You're good to go, boss," Roach yelled.

Swash stomped on the accelerator as the final four marauder trucks, accompanied by overhead gun drones, came around the corner. He took direct aim at the first gasser. The head-on collision would send the petrol engine straight into his lap.

A blast from Blade split the vehicle in two, crashing the remains into its companions. The Beast plowed full speed through the wreckage. Flames, screeching metal, and ominous pounding from the undercarriage sent the Beast on its three inline starboard wheels.

"That one hurt," Roach yelled through the com set as the rover returned to the ground.

"She's stronger than she looks." Swash had seen the Beast endure far worse than a little bumping and grinding.

"Tell that to my plasma readout." Blade jerked on the

cannon. "Somebody'd better check those batteries, because I know I didn't fire off three-quarters of our power."

Stitch struggled through the hatch toward Swash, holding onto every railing she could grab hold of. "You seem to need a little help up here."

"You should be strapped in." Swash didn't have time for a medical analysis of their situation.

She knelt down at his side. "All forward batteries are reading zero, midships are twenty-five percent, and aft gauges are swinging wildly."

"Strap in, Stitch. That's an order." He couldn't afford to have their medic get bounced into a coma.

She fumbled for the center observation chair. "This is bad, isn't it?"

"Don't be silly. Bad is still somewhere over the horizon." Swash's grandfather had used that throwaway comment in difficult situations, invariably followed by some ill-advised adventure.

2

The Beast continued to lumber through the T-Hatch Mountains. Though they'd managed to blast out of the low canyons, they weren't out of danger. Swash wouldn't feel comfortable until he'd put a warlord's territory between the Beast and Scorch's attack force, and that meant heading out of the Californias for the territories of the great desert.

With the rest of the crew grabbing some much-needed rest, he lounged in the driver's chair with the rover set on autopilot drone control. So long as nothing larger than a desert rat jumped into their path, he could afford to stare lazily at the view screen and contemplate how it was that he was still alive. From what Swash's father had told him, Jones had been a common name at one time. But then, common men were often the first sent into battle. To be a Jones and to have survived the Wars of Divergence was a major accomplishment—a heritage to be proud of. He doubted there were more than a dozen Joneses left in all of North America.

The name Swash had been his mother's idea. The woman had spent far too much time romanticizing about the past. Some people just didn't belong in the twenty-third century, and Meadow Jones had been one of them—nostalgic and naive. Swash wondered how the woman had lasted as long as she had. All he had to remember her by was his name. Surviving in a tin can on wheels with a crew of four to take care of while roaming the desolation of North America wasn't an arrangement that encouraged hanging onto sentimental keepsakes.

"Captain, I need you to see this." Whisper's voice from the communication room adjoining the bridge brought Swash out of his half sleep.

Swash bristled at being called *Captain*. Invariably, it meant there was a problem. At least when Roach called him *boss*, it was in good-natured ribbing. Being the captain was too much like being the janitor. He was only called in when there was shit to clean up.

With the Beast's hand throttle set at one-half speed and nothing but empty desert ahead, he realized he'd nodded off with his hand still on the wheel. "I'm a little busy." He jerked the wheel to prove to the rest on board that he was doing his job at the helm.

The mousy girl, who seemed to always pop up at the worst moments, stuck her head through the hatch. "It's important."

Swash could fight his way out of an enemy tavern after having out-drunk and out-whored the best of the marauders. When it came to knowing what was over the next ridge, however, he—and every other driver—was completely at a loss without drone support. And much as he hated to admit it, Whisper had proven to be one of the best drone operators he'd encountered. That bought her the benefit of civility even when he wanted to bite her head off for the disturbance.

He leaned back in the worn military chair. "So tell me."

Whisper pulled off the virtual-reality goggles and earphone that covered half of her face. "It's a bird. Transstat 887."

Swash leaned his head back over the driver's chair. When he'd agreed to let her power up the old roof-mounted satellite dish, he'd known it would bite him in the ass one day. "I thought all of those things were just space debris."

Every war story he'd heard from his grandfather had involved some form of technological duplicity, usually involving fake GPS readings or false imaging. The old man had used *satellites* as a swear word as often as *fracking*. Either term, shouted or grumbled by his grandfather while in the captain's chair, meant trouble on the horizon.

"A lot of them were destroyed, but mostly, that's what the key holders want you to believe," Whisper said.

Tired, he wasn't in the mood for a bedtime story. "There's no superior technology floating around overhead. Not anymore. Whatever tin cans are left up there are only filled with the lies of politicians."

"You're a true scholar, aren't you?"

The insult made Swash reach for his knife. Scholars had

been the ones who'd gotten the world into the mess it was in. "I won't stand for being insulted, not on my own rig."

Whisper raised her hands. "I didn't mean anything by it. My mother is a key holder, so I do have some insight into those tin cans."

"Okay. So tell me—who are these key holders you talk about?"

She plopped down in the navigator's chair and turned it toward him. "Before the wars really got fired up, some individuals realized the dangers the satellites represented. With the correct access, a person could locate anyone on the planet, manipulate information, and even delete data from ground-based computers. All information wasn't just routed through the orbiting birds—it was held onto like a fish on a line. As the satellites fell into the hands of hackers, there were some interspace battles. If those in power couldn't retrieve their birds, they'd just as soon no one else had them. It didn't take many battles before the hackers realized the real trick was stealing satellites without anyone knowing."

Swash was already getting bored. History was for children and chumps. "So... what? They flew up there, stuck a tow hook to the bird, and dragged it into another orbit?"

"It was simpler than that. All a hacker needed to do was fire up the positioning rockets. Of course, once the bird was moved, they had to cover their tracks. Since every piece of space junk was very accurately identified, all they could do to hide the theft was turn off the bird. With all of the debris up there, it was usually assumed the satellite had been hit."

Swash imagined the sky filled with garbage. "But if the bird's turned off, what's the point in stealing it?"

Whisper reached over and turned her desk light on then off again. "You can turn them on. Typically, a bird gets fired up, information is downloaded, then the bird gets turned off again. Every hacker has their own system, but there's always a key. It could be a code or a number—really, anything that the satellite will notice. Hackers will only use their birds when they think no one is looking, and then only for short bursts of time."

Swash really wanted to return to his sleep driving. "The wars ended fifty years ago. Those hackers must be dying off by now."

"And that's were the key master comes in. No one knows who he is or how he figured things out, but he's been collecting satellites."

Swash rubbed his eyes. It had been one hell of a day, and thinking made him nauseous. "What does this have to do with anything?"

"As I said, my mother is a key holder. She inherited the bird from her father."

"And?" He wished she'd get to the point.

"Though I grew up in the mountains, Mother kept her base a secret even from me. I only had part of the coordinates. The message she just sent me is the remaining number. I've already checked my maps. The location is high in the Rocky Mountains."

"You must be crazy if you think I'm driving the Beast up those ridges. Why can't we meet her someplace more accessible?"

Whisper opened the long wide drawer under the now quiet holographic drone display and pulled out a large yellowed topographical map. "The higher you go, the more sky you can listen to, and that means the more birds you can find. Mom has spent her life cataloging every live bird she hears. She wouldn't call me home unless it was important."

"Sounds like her daughter suffers from the same affliction."

Whisper continued as if Swash hadn't made the comment. "I know I'm in no position to ask any favors. I owe you my freedom as well as my life. Please, Swash, we have to go up there."

Swash thought the whole thing sounded like another of the girl's romantic delusions. "If her request is so dang important that she used her bird, why didn't she just send a message? Sending a number could mean anything."

"She can never be sure who else is listening."

Blindly following a message from space was a good way of getting snared. "How do you know it was even her? Maybe it's this key master dude. Did you think of that? We could be walking into a trap."

"If it is, that's all the more reason to go."

Swash stared at the mountain range barely visible on the great desert's horizon. The roads that had once been cut to climb the cliffs and ridges had mostly been demolished during the wars. Those people who remained in the high up were none too fond of visitors. And from their vantage point, they could unleash a barrage of rocks, creating avalanches even the Beast couldn't withstand. "Risky. How do you even know she's up there?"

"She knows I'm listening. She wouldn't fire up our bird unless I was close. I don't often ask to go somewhere, but this is important."

And possibly lucrative? With Scorch turning the Californias into territories, Swash could no longer do business. He needed to either find abandoned settlements to raid and outposts willing to barter with an unknown rover or figure out another way to keep his crew fed. Neither option was likely to be found in the great desert.

Roach poked his head through the hatch. "That's thirty hours, boss. Stitch's orders, you need some rest."

Swash got up and put his hand on Whisper's shoulder. "I'm not agreeing to anything, but for now, we don't have much of a choice but to head in that direction. We'll talk later."

3

*S*wash collapsed onto his bunk and pulled the drum shut. The time before sleep was the worst. His routine was to work a good solid thirty hours before succumbing to the bodily requirement. Stitch refused to let him stay on the bridge any longer than that, and much to Swash's dismay, the rest of the crew diligently enforced her command. So long as he could work his way into a semicatatonic state, he had a shot at not tossing in the bunk for the eight hours of required time off.

"Apocalyptic depression," the med heads called it. Technically, it wasn't a treatable condition, since every sane person on the planet suffered from it.

How could they not? he'd wondered after the initial diagnosis. The planet was toast. And not the nice lightly browned kind that you could slather with melted butter and jam. No. The planet was the kind of toast that set off fire alarms and came out looking like the charred remains of an animal that had been flattened by a truck then forced between the electric coils.

A laugh formed in Swash's chest that failed to make it up to his throat. The medics had explained that a warped sense of humor was a potential side effect of apocalyptic depression. Staring into the abyss of what mankind had destroyed, he could either jump in or go full manic, but only the truly deranged succumbed to either extreme.

"Not today." He rolled over in the metal tube. There would be another day of what Earth's man-made hell had to offer.

A red light and quiet buzzing roused him from his contemplation. "What?" At least the crew had learned not to hammer on the metal to get him up. Being in the bunk was like sleeping in a steel drum.

"Sorry, boss," Roach said over the intercom. "I've got something you might want to see."

At the rate he'd been going, sleep would have still been a good three hours away. Swash was glad for the distraction. Yanking on the handle, he remembered the last time he'd snuck out of bed. "Tell Stitch to turn off the goddamn time lock."

The metal side slid up. "Did you sleep?" Stitch curled her bare toes, lifting the soles of her feet off of the metal-plate floor. She shivered in her nightgown.

"I was in there for all of five minutes. What do you think?"

She checked the digital clock over the hatch to the bridge. "You were in there for five hours. I'll take that as a positive sign. No stimulants today, okay?"

Frack you, Stitch, Swash thought. "No promises until I talk to Roach. If we're coming apart at the seams, I'll need more than a caffeine bar. What are the readings outside?" Roach's problems almost always involved coming to a stop and dealing with nature's ungodly elements.

"Winds blowing north to south, so no radiation threat. Much as I hate the desert, I've yet to come across a virus that can handle the hot dry of the open plain."

Swash had never encountered a virus in the desert either. It was almost as if nature believed the intense heat was enough of a challenge for the living to deal with. He sat up on the edge of his berth. "Sorry about my attitude. Guess I'm not a morning person."

She half smiled. "I've gotten used to it. What can we expect out there?"

"This never was a food-growing region, so I'd expect the agrochemical contamination to be minimal."

Stitch pulled her translucent wrap tighter around her body. "The environment isn't leaving us much to work with, and I still need that Iodine-X to treat Blade."

She was right. The hydro collectors in the air intakes hadn't gathered more than a cup of water in last four days. He didn't want to ask about the food provisions. They were heading out into complete desolation with practically nothing in reserve. "Tell me the truth. Do you think it was a mistake starting off across the desert?" The fact that Swash was even asking her opinion was proof that he hadn't had enough sleep.

"I'd say yes, but that would assume we had another choice."

Swash swung down from the bunk. "Hopefully, Roach has some good news."

She touched his arm as she walked past him to her bunk right behind his in the med unit. "I'll put on something more decent and meet you on the bridge."

When Swash pushed through the hatch, Roach sat up in the driver's chair. "I might have something, boss."

Swash fell into the navigator's chair. "Talk to me."

Roach activated the hologram on the dashboard desk between the two bridge stations. The three-dimensional map showed the Beast sitting on the rim overlooking a bowl-shaped valley. In the middle of the playa lay a tumble of decaying buildings. "The hummingbird caught this, so I pulled under a sand cliff and shut down. Before rousing you out of bed, I searched Whisper's supply of antique paper maps. Apparently, it was a small city. That's about all I've got."

"It's something at least."

Swash was becoming desperate for supplies to raid. Their run from the Islands of Lost Angels had nearly drained their fuel tank. Though they could solar up during the day and creep along at night, the photocells wouldn't do much good if they ran into a sandstorm—or worse, marauders. That was assuming they still had fully functional batteries, which according to the gauges was not the case. Ultimately, he was going to need the multifuel engines, and probably sooner rather than later.

He leaned over the display. "Any signs of life?" Though it was two in the morning, in the desert, where daytime temperatures could reach into the mid-one-hundreds, people had a way of turning nocturnal.

"Not that I can see, but the drone was set for autopilot a half mile ahead of the Beast, so there wasn't the ability to make multiple passes. Soon as I shut down, it came sailing home, and I woke you."

Stitch stepped onto the bridge, pulling a more discreet robe around her. "Why have we stopped?"

Swash waved at the display. "Potential provisions. What's your initial medical impression?"

She studied the hologram. "Too far away for me to give clearance. Radiation should be okay, but there could be pathogens."

He stared at the paper map and concluded that he would need to wake the others. Though sleep was a demon that fought him at every toss and turn, that wasn't the case for everyone in his crew. "I hate to do it, but you'd better get Whisper out of her pod. Might as well hammer on Blade's cylinder as well. I'm going to want everyone's assessment before deciding if the risk is worth the reward."

THE BEAST'S main bridge seated two comfortably and three reasonably. With two people standing, all five members of the crew could fit in a pinch. Though the living quarters, with its eight sleeping cylinders and bolted-down protective chairs, made more sense for meetings, all too often something on the bridge's holographic display was the topic under discussion.

By the time Whisper and Blade joined the party, Swash knew what he had to do. "I'm sending in the magpie drone. We need air readings and soil samples so Stitch can work up a medical-risk analysis. I'd like to get a slow pass down Main Street to see what kind of security was left behind."

"Assuming it was left behind." For big man adept at taking care of himself, Blade had an annoying habit of expecting the worst. "A slow pass by that big bird could call in all kinds of trouble. We could skirt the rim and be on our way."

"And go where, Blade?" Stitch glared up at the man. "Did you forget about your firefight through that canyon? If I don't get some Iodine-X into you by the end of the day, you'll be risking cancer, or worse."

"I feel fine."

She shook her head. "We're also running low on water and biomaterial. The photosynthesizer needs *something* to work on." Stitch knew exactly how to set Blade off and was always goading the big man.

From his ramrod stance against the bulkhead, it was clear Blade had understood her insinuation. "I'm not eating reconstituted shit."

"No one's saying we're going to feed the black pellets into the food generator," Swash said. "Those things are worth way too much to the agrocamps."

Blade remained next to the door as if guarding it from anyone with any funny ideas. "I'm just saying I'm not eating reconstituted shit."

"Yes. We heard you the first time." Stitch turned toward Swash, hiding her smile of satisfaction from Blade.

"It's not just a matter of food." Roach tapped the fuel gauges. "With the damage to the batteries, we're going to have to rely more on the multifuel engines, but we're down to a quarter tank of plant oil." At least he hadn't mentioned the empty go-juice tank. Their run down the mountain escaping raiders had drained the high-octane brew that could propel the Beast to speeds high enough to outflank attackers if not outrun them.

"Whisper, outfit the magpie," Swash said. "I want a full medical assessment before anyone goes in. Blade, watch the holographic drone display and direct Whisper. We need to identify which buildings are the most likely to contain biological material. If all looks good, we'll send in the jump spider at dawn. If anyone is hiding out down there, they won't want to get into a fight that drags into the heat of day."

"You don't want to send in the Beast?" Roach asked.

Though they could strip the town clean with the storage space that the Beast would provide, Swash was reluctant to send the vehicle in. He was having that whole-body itchy feeling that told him to be cautious. "Not initially. If the jump spider comes back without encountering any issues and finds what we need, then we'll swoop in. If all goes according to plan, I'd like to set up somewhere soon so we can process some juice."

An audible excitement filled the room. Making go-juice meant breaking out the still. Not all alcohol was destined for the engines.

4

---

*S*titch sat on the metal chair behind the swing-out table. Every crew member had a little private corner of the Beast. Roach had his mechanic's workshop and Whisper her radio alcove off the bridge. Blade made his escapes out back to sit in the jump spider—the all-terrain vehicle—for a little alone time, and Stitch had her medical center. The room wasn't much larger than a closet, but with its retractable walls, it was environmentally sealed off from the rest of the living space. And with her bunk above and a patient bunk below, she could keep an eye on anyone needing isolation.

She set the concentrated air samples from the magpie in her rapid-growth incubator. The news was bad. That was obvious from the sickly-green med filters ejected from the drone at her feet. Had it not been for the bacteria-resistant polymer coating every inch of the flying machine, she'd have tossed the whirlybird into the decontamination vat without ever letting it on board the Beast.

The inoculant generator sitting next to the incubator was simple enough to operate. Once enough of the nasty life-threating microorganisms were harvested and rapidly aged to near death, the sample could be added to the standard fare of medications. Really, all Stitch had to do was transfer the materials while not letting anything escape. So long as the pathogen wasn't mutating faster than the away team's mission, everyone should be okay.

She pulled out the box of medical masks. Relying on anything to remain stable was just asking for trouble. It was always better to have a backup plan.

"How's it looking?" Swash asked from outside of the medical closet.

"I'll have the injections within the hour. I'm making up enough for everyone."

"How long can we stay in that environment?"

She could hear the anxiousness in his voice. *How long?* was always the big question and one she could only guess at. Unless the sample started mutating before her eyes, there was really no way to know for sure. According to her education, viruses were supposed to take months or even years to evolve, not days or hours. But such was the world she lived in. Inoculations were like the proverbial Chinese food—soon after taking them, a person would be back for more.

"I wouldn't push it past sundown. And if anyone sees any recently dead carcasses out there, call the mission off."

"You're the expert. I defer to your superior education."

The ding of the computer egg timer corresponded to only a slight yellowing around the edge of the sample. "Tenacious little devils, aren't you?" She advanced the aging processor to a factor of ten. On the electron-microscope screen, she watched the monsters struggle to outgrow their destruction. "Don't feel bad, little cruddies. Right now, I expect some higher being is doing to us exactly what I'm doing to you."

WITH THE INOCULATIONS ADMINISTERED, Stitch inspected each of the crew's biohazard overalls. "Keep them as snug as you can stand. I don't want any pathogens sneaking their way inside."

"I don't see why I need to wear this thing." Roach struggled to get the head-to-toe garment to fit properly. "I'm just the guy behind the wheel. Blade and Whisper are the only ones going in."

Swash checked the flexibility of the suit's arms. "We're all wearing them, Roach, so get used to it. If something happens out there, we have to be ready to rush in for the rescue."

"What can we expect if it tears?" Blade fit his blaster's holster around the leg of the bodysuit.

"If you get cut, expect a week of excruciating pain and vomiting if you're lucky. Keep the medical tape handy. The sooner you prevent infection, the easier it will be for me to save your life." She handed over the two medical masks. "Put these under your face cowlings. They'll get a little warm from your breathing, but it should buy you some time if everything else fails."

"You're not making me feel at ease." Whisper snugged the mask around her face before picking up the metal and agroleather half face shield that would protect her from the sand.

Swash stood straight as if indicating that the time for discussion had ended. "We need supplies. It's that simple. Without biomass and water, we won't survive the trip across the desert. The likelihood of finding another town for easier pickings is slim to none. This section of North America never was heavily populated. Get in. Get what we need. Get out. And don't get hurt. The sooner you're done, the sooner we can get out of this environmental skillet."

Stitch watched Roach, Blade, and Whisper head out the door to test the bodysuits in the desert air and prepare the jump spider. "I've done all I can."

Swash patted her on the back. "You never really get used to the feeling of helplessness."

5

*B*lade didn't dislike Whisper—not really. Sure, she got on his nerves like an annoying baby sister who kept creating trouble but never got reprimanded for it. She was too smart for her own good and mischievous in getting what she wanted out of Swash, and she had cockamamie ideas about damn near everything. Half of the time she made him laugh, and the other half she spent pissing him off. There was no middle ground with her. When it came to away missions, though, she had her skills. He surveyed the desert. Somewhere just beyond the sand dunes was bounty or danger—or most likely, both.

Out on the catwalk, Whisper kicked him on the shin. "Are you going to get the jump spider ready or just stare at the horizon all day?"

Though she annoyed him, he knew how to get under her skin as well. "Why do you even want to go? Wouldn't you rather stay here and play with your antenna set?"

"It's not a toy," Whisper said from between clenched teeth. "You need me. I can sneak into spaces you'd have to blast apart to get that fat ass into."

"I didn't ask what use you'd be." He leaned in so Roach, who was on the ground below, wouldn't hear. "I saw the antique store."

She raised her head. "Hey, those items are useful. Based on the level of technology of the stuff we spotted, I'd say that town's been empty for a hundred years. I know that's a long time, but it sure beats some of the other settlements we've run across. I just want to take a peek in the stores if we get a chance."

"Right." Blade didn't believe her for an instant. Anything Whisper tried to sneak aboard, however, was Swash's problem. "Ground rules." He waited for her to recite them.

She let out a loud sigh. The sound and accompanying eye roll would have been more appropriate for a teenager than a woman in her midtwenties. "We leave the moment you tell me, no delays. The jump spider doesn't have much storage, so I can only take what I can carry on my body."

He stared at her, wondering if she'd really forgotten his most important command. "And if I whistle?"

"I hide and don't do anything stupid."

He never could tell whether she was being serious or sarcastic. "I mean it, Whisper. These away missions are dangerous. If we get jumped, I can't risk the safety of the crew by searching for you. I'll get in the vehicle and head out for the desert to lead our assailant away from the Beast. You'll be on your own. When I swing back, you'd better be where I left you. So if you don't want to get left behind, fracking stay close this time!"

"Just get the damn jump spider down from the Beast."

He stepped through the hatch to the engine bay while she descended the stairs to the sand. He unlatched the square metal door from the back wall of the Beast and swung it out of the way. The access was barely large enough for him to fit through.

He reached up, grabbed the overhead bar, and swung his legs through the square hole. It took four-limb dexterity to land upside down on the jump spider's driver's seat. Roach had made it look easy. Too easy. Blade's back still ached when he thought about his early attempts. The question of how the pilot mechanic was able to contort his body into every unimaginably tight space wasn't one Blade wanted to pursue. He just wished the guy would come along on an away mission or two.

After flipping the switch to light up the electronics, Blade checked the fuel gauge. One-quarter of a tank wasn't going to get him far, but he might have enough range to distract a contingent of marauders.

"What's taking so long?" Whisper asked.

The same energy that made her jumpy to get on with the mission had Blade rechecking his weapons. "Grab another battery pack from Roach. I've only got two on board. Do you still have that knife I gave you?"

"Of course."

Blade didn't need to see her to know she was rolling her eyes again. He opened the fuel petcock then gave the thumb pump a couple of good pushes to ensure the carburetor was primed. To keep the vehicle as light and versatile as possible, the technology had been kept pretty basic. With the punch of a button he had the small engine purring. "Releasing. Watch out below."

He stomped on the release lever, and the jump spider fell backward out of the shoot at the back of the Beast. The instant the back tires hit the sand and the fronts were clear of the overhang, Blade tapped the gas, landing the vehicle right side up. In its fully lowered configuration, the jump spider's five-foot-diameter tires extended above and below the two-person rail-frame cab.

Whisper reached over the top and handed him the spare battery pack along with a shopping list of items requested from the rest of the crew. "Swash wants us to bring a storage drum. He says the more biomass we find, the better. Along with the Iodine-X, Stitch has some meds she'd like us to search for if possible. And Roach would appreciate any steel-bar stock we run across."

Blade would have resented the fifty-five-gallon attachment had it not meant the possibility of a jar of hooch when Swash was done making go-juice. As for the rest of the stuff, well, he wasn't playing Santa Claus on this trip. He folded the page until only the Iodine-X was visible. The potential of finding biomass was even money. Any rotting food could be converted by the photosynthesizer, which meant so long as the cans, jars, and boxes hadn't busted open and their contents turned to dust, the crew had a reasonable expectation of success. As for water, any liquid they found, no matter how putrid, could be purified into something drinkable. When it came to finding actually edible food, Blade set the odds at somewhere south of a hundred to one. The chance of locating Stitch's extensive wish list of medical supplies was closer to a thousand to one. Even if they did find an infirmary, the likelihood that any of the meds would still be usable after a hundred years was nothing more than wishful thinking. Not that it mattered.

It's not your fault that they're dead. He shook his head to shut down the refrain before it could take over his thoughts and memories, and he refocused on the mission.

Blade twisted the wheel and backed the jump spider to the low-hanging drum. With a pull of the rack handle, Whisper dropped the container onto the jump spider's curved supports. She climbed up the back, secured the straps to the drum, then plopped down through the open roof onto the passenger's seat. "I'll never understand why Roach didn't think this thing needed doors."

"With the size of these tires? How would they open?" Without waiting for an answer, Blade stepped on the long accelerator lever, sending sand flying from all four wheels.

In its lowered stance, the jump spider could fly over the ground and jump any hurdle with ease. The front and bottom cowling diverted most of the stinging white sand, but no one would ever mistake the ride for being comfortable. He laid into the go-juice, jumped a dune, and landed ten feet away.

"You're not joyriding out there." Swash's voice over the headset brought Blade back to his mission.

"Sorry." Blade would have promised it wouldn't happen again, but that would have been an outright lie.

He laid off the throttle until the sand rooster tails from the tires had subsided below the level of the dunes. There wasn't any advantage to letting the potential enemy know they were coming. The magpie hadn't indicated anyone was home, but the big-ass drone wasn't exactly inconspicuous.

Whisper pointed toward a mound of sand that looked like every other mound of sand. "It should be on the other side of that dune."

Instead of circling around on the relatively hard surface, he aimed the jump spider at the incline and dug the tires into the soft sand. Halfway up, he shut off the motor.

"What are you doing?" she asked.

He reached up to the roll bar and hauled himself off the seat. "I want to get a look before we go balls-deep into trouble."

"We already *had* a look. That's what the magpie was about."

"*You* had a look. I'll be right back. Keep your ass in that chair." He couldn't calculate their odds of survival without a better idea of what they were walking into.

As he climbed, his boots, which laced halfway up his leg, sank into the loose sand like the dune was trying to eat him. At the top, he lay flat and pulled out his binoculars. The decaying structures resembled the bleached bones of some long-dead creature—one that no one remembered or cared had gone extinct. Herding people together onto squared-off sections of land, having them cower in rooms like livestock waiting to be butchered, then wondering why the criminal element crept in like wolves into a henhouse was just frack-head behavior. He scanned the streets and storefronts for any wayward soul who'd managed to survive whatever onslaught had decimated the place. Sand filled every right angle, from street to curb and sidewalk to building wall, as if to say people were idiots for squaring nature. The sand was right. People were idiots. But just because the small granules had taken over, that didn't mean some menace wasn't lurking under the white powder.

"What do you see?" Whisper lay down next to him. He hadn't even realized she'd left the jump spider. The girl might be annoying, but she had mad skills when it came to being sneaky.

"What did I tell you?"

"To stay put, but we both knew that wasn't going to happen. So what's out there? Anything good?" She put her hands under her chin and gazed out at the ruins.

He turned back to his binoculars. "The obvious sources for food look pretty ransacked. Not a surprise, but if we don't find something better, we'll check them out anyway. Petroleum stations are nothing more than craters. Whoever siphoned off the last of the gasoline didn't want anyone else sopping up the remains." Blade couldn't resist shaking his head at the absurdity of making fuel out of something sucked out of the ground. *You can't even drink the stuff.*

Whisper shrugged. "It's not like Swash would let that black tar into the Beast's tanks anyway."

She was right. Besides, the stuff had a stench to it that made Blade want to retch, not that he'd admit that weakness to Whisper. "Your antique store has the windows smashed in, but there's still crap inside."

She silently clapped her hands. "We need to find biomass

first, or the captain won't let me bring my bounty aboard. Any places that might have medical supplies?"

He scanned the less commercial streets. Going dwelling to dwelling was slow business, but during the final days of a city, people found unique ways of hiding their provisions, and Whisper excelled at worming her way into the hidden cellars. "The buildings on the western edge of town look to have been the last to be deserted. Being this close to the nuclear trench, we might get lucky. Disease and radiation tend to make people hightail it out of town without worrying about what they were leaving behind."

She hunched closer as if trying to peer through the binoculars. "What do you see in the way of life?"

"It's like staring into a city of the dead. There's not even a cockroach scurrying around out there."

She grabbed the binoculars while the strap was still around his neck. "We need to find something useful."

Still collared by the strap like a dog, he turned to her. "Then I'm afraid we're down to door-to-door scavenging."

She handed back the binoculars before scooching down the slope on her belly. When she was well below the ridge, she stood without the threat of being noticed from town. "Then we'd better get moving."

BACK IN THE JUMP SPIDER, Blade flared the wheel-rim supports and raised the rear of the cab. Acting like an old-time side paddlewheel ship, the vehicle powered back up over the sand and descended the slope. On the hard pack, he raised the front to match the back and returned the wheel blades to their interlocking defense position.

"I want to start in the western neighborhood closest to the school." Whisper pulled the hood of her coveralls over her head, indicating she was getting down to business.

Deciding where to hunt was a team effort. Dangerous areas like the center of town were usually his prerogative, while the more residential areas were better understood by Whisper. "Just tell me it's not because the antique store is close by."

She continued snugging up her outfit until there wasn't a stray flap along either arms or legs. "No, silly. People who had children went through food faster, so there was usually more on hand. Schools were also often refuges of last resort. If we can't find your Iodine-X in a home, we'll check out the school's medical stash."

He kept the jump spider in the freshly blown sand while skirting the edge of town. With the sun still below the surrounding hills, he didn't want to risk getting caught in an unseen wheel trap. She must have sensed his increased vigilance, because she'd stopped talking. When it came to putting on their game faces and getting serious about the mission, they worked well together.

He slowed as he spotted the wide-open field with rusting posts at either end. "Pick a street."

Her eyes peered over the mouth-and-nose mask, scanning the neighborhood. She pointed haphazardly at the nearest block of houses. "Those look okay."

In spite of the smashed windows, the first couple of buildings didn't seem too far gone. "I'll head a block in then we'll start. Marauders like hitting the perimeter buildings, but if the sickness was as bad as Stitch said, they would have avoided going farther into the neighborhoods."

The tires of the jump spider hit the concrete roadway under a thin layer of sand. The jolt made Blade wince. The thing never felt right running on solid surfaces—too rumbly. He kept the speed down and inspected every building like it was an enemy's stronghold.

After passing through the intersection, he pulled the jump spider into the yard of a two-story house. "I'll go in first."

Whisper nodded without unbuckling her seatbelt. When it came to honest danger, she could behave when she wanted to. "Don't get hurt." The phrase was one she said to him on every incursion.

He pulled the plasma blaster from the hard-plastic sleeve against his thigh. Before leaving the jump spider, he made sure it was comfortably idling. "If you leave—"

"Shut it off. I know."

He scampered out the top and jumped to the ground. Either the desert house had been built to mesh with its surroundings, or the wind-driven sand had softened its edges—he couldn't tell. As he walked past the garage, he ran his finger along the paper-thin pane of glass. It was still intact—a good sign nothing had been disturbed. Whoever had designed the garish wooden front door and carved an oriental motif into it clearly hadn't been the same person who'd designed the structure. He gave a firm shoulder strike, and the dried wood of the doorframe crumbled to splinters—another good sign that no one had been in the place. If pillaging marauders had been there, the door would have been caved in already.

Stepping into the main living space was like walking into a time capsule. The carpet disintegrated under his boots. A gust of wind sneaked through the door behind him and teased the drapes. The movement was enough to cause them to shatter into a cloud of flying polyester flakes.

He tapped the com that snaked from his ear to his mouth. "Pull the ignition module from the jump spider and come in. There isn't so much as a ghost living here." Despite the fact that the place seemed deserted, he kept his blaster at the ready. Bait wasn't supposed to reveal the hook, and he wasn't about to play the big dumb fish.

Whisper snuck in on her all-cloth shoes. The stupid things looked like booties, but they made her all but silent. He knew the white overalls weren't her favorite, but with the impending blast of sunlight, she'd fry to a crisp in the black agroleathers she preferred wearing while stealing stuff. "I'm not so sure about those ghosts. I can practically hear their feet whooshing through the carpet threads."

Though not prone to childish fears, Blade knew what she meant. "Be careful, okay?"

"I'll follow your lead."

6

Whisper liked Blade more than she wanted to admit. He was big and strong and confident and manly. No one gave him crap about anything. Not that her feelings were sexual. When it came to intercourse, she could take it or leave it. The physical interlocking of body parts was okay—it was the noises that bothered her. People sounded like rutting animals while they were getting it on, and that reminded her of how people actually had been animals. They weren't anymore. An animal population instinctively knew when it had damaged its environment. People didn't have a clue. They just kept on popping out babies like there was a world left for them to live in. The thought pattern wasn't conducive to achieving orgasm.

No. Her feelings for Blade didn't run toward the physical. He made her feel safe, and that wasn't something she could say about many men she'd met in her life. As she snuck into the kitchen with him standing guard, she knew she wouldn't have to keep checking over her shoulder for some creeper. That was the luxury of going on a mission with Blade. The man would fight to his last breath to give her time to escape. It wasn't that she was special to him; he'd do it for any member of the crew.

She eased an upper cabinet open with the tips of her fingers. Even if most of the city was bathed in pathogens, rodents had a way of surviving. "Lots of dust and plastic remnants," she said quietly into the headset. "Hard to say how much is from the cabinet interior and how much from long-gone foodstuff." She pulled on a long string of clear plastic that tore like peeling skin.

"Do we move on to the next house?" Blade asked. For all of his bravado, when it came to scavenging he relied on her expertise. Each time he asked for her advice, she got a warm feeling in the center of her chest.

"Not yet." She bent down to the lower doors. Again, she teased them open without disturbing the layer of dust that mounded on top of the thin wood. Stacks of pots and pans not that dissimilar to what she remembered as a child lay on the shelves as if ready to be used for the nightly meal. "Everything is too well preserved for there not to be something worth taking."

"Do you want me to help look?"

She held a reverence for unmolested places like this one. Perhaps it was foolish—Blade had certainly told her that enough times—but she felt she owed something to history. Turning the big man loose would leave the house in ruins. "No, thanks. I'm going to look for a basement."

"There are some stairs off the living room."

She nodded to herself. "Give me a minute to check the rest of these cabinets, then I'll head down. When I give you the all clear, check the upstairs bathrooms for medical supplies. We need that Iodine-X."

"Yes, Mother." Blade never could adequately pull off the sarcastic tone—his voice was just too deep and masculine—but that didn't stop him from trying.

With every cabinet and drawer open and nothing to show for it, Whisper backed out of the kitchen. "I won't be long. If I don't find anything, we'll move on to the next house."

She pulled out the ignition box from her overalls then handed it to him as she walked through the main living space, just in case something bad happened. She held the banisters and eased her weight onto the first stair. Though buildings could stand for hundreds of years, they could crumble in on themselves at the first new inhabitant. It was like they were doing all they could to hold it together, but once they were once again put to use, they just lost it.

The wood was firmer than she'd expected. At the bottom, she pulled out her flashlight. "Looks like it was some kind of entertainment room."

"Any hooch?"

She aimed the beam at the corner. Her heart doubled its beating. "Glass bottles, most of them still with liquid inside."

"I'm coming down."

She would have been powerless to stop him. "Just don't break anything." It was amazing to her that people took such care with alcohol. Glass was the one material that never showed the effects of age. She crept around a large table with what she assumed were pocketed holes for drinks, though it would have been for a huge banquet with so much space between slots and requiring such a large support structure. "There must be food around here somewhere."

Blade didn't even bother reading the labels or checking the contents. He stashed bottles in every pocket then filled his arms until he couldn't hold one more bottle. "I'm going to run these upstairs. Don't go getting distracted. We still need organic material for the photosynthesizer."

"Look who's talking," she muttered.

While he struggled upstairs with his cache, she continued on to the skinny door next to the bar. She'd just gotten the age-sealed door open when she heard his whistle of alarm. *Dammit, Blade. I knew you should have stayed on guard upstairs and not come down for the hooch.* She wedged her way into the room and pulled the door shut. Hopefully, he'd just seen something he didn't like or was testing her resolve. She listened intently for the sound of the jump spider speeding away. Unfortunately, that was exactly what she heard.

WHISPER KNEW HER LIMITATIONS. She was a hider, not a fighter. After a quick scan of the pantry and all of its wonders, she turned off the flashlight and huddled in the corner behind a stack of plastic crates. The room would give Stitch everything she needed to provide food for the crew, if Whisper ever got out. She rubbed the dust off of a big red cross on the white crate in front of her. *Medical stuff. Stitch will be pleased.* She didn't dare hope there might be something still edible among the cans and jars on the shelves. Real food was a luxury she hadn't experienced in months. She couldn't blame Blade for fixating on the hooch. Telling him about it had been a mistake, but she doubted she'd have been able to keep it a secret for long.

The emergency plan was simple. Blade would hop in the jump spider and lead the pursuers away from their treasure, but to make sure he had everyone, he'd make a pass or two through the neighborhood. She had to resist the urge to dive for the vehicle when he flew by. If their enemy didn't think anyone was left behind, they'd remain focused on Blade. Once he was confident he had everyone accounted for, he'd head out into the desert. Nothing beat the jump spider when it came to climbing sand dunes. While leading the chase, he'd get word to Swash. When Blade had the marauders cleared from town, the Beast would swoop in and pick her up—along with as many supplies as they dared hustle aboard. Then, if Blade hadn't already bogged all of the chase vehicles in the sand, the Beast would close in behind the bastards and save him. All Whisper had to do was listen for the Beast.

She closed her eyes to focus on what she heard. Sounds were her friends. No matter how confusing life got, she could always count on the truth of sounds. The wind rasped the sand against the stucco siding, tapped it against the window glass like the feet of a thousand insects, and let out a swirling howl between the buildings. As she concentrated on nature's music, it became like a voice telling her everything was okay from its perspective.

As with listening to a symphony, she needed a moment to pick out the subtler instruments. A colony of wood-burrowing insects was diligently gnawing away at the building's structure. From the firm chomps, she assumed the buggies hadn't been there long. *Interesting. I wonder where they came from? Probably the insect version of human marauders, moving from house to house once the previous supplies were exhausted.*

She didn't need to feel the heat to know the sun had crested the mountains. Based on the rapid, crisp expansion pops of clay tiles resting on the roof's wooden beams, it was going to be a hot one. Just like every other day in the desert.

As if admitting defeat in the game of waiting out the other, a rat started his reconnaissance on the shelf above her. She'd always hated the little monsters. *Tap, tap, sniff. Tap, tap, sniff. Could you fracking be more obvious in your search?* He had her. The only question was who would draw first blood. She eased the knife Blade had given her out from the side-leg pocket of her bodysuit. Though Whisper played the frightened animal in staying quiet and, hopefully, unobserved, she saw herself more as a snake lying in wait. Unfortunately for the rat, he didn't seem the type to leave her be.

The sound of scampering little claws on metal shelving announced his attack. Though she couldn't see much in the dark, she didn't really need to. With a firm, backhanded slash, she cut the bastard's throat just as he dove toward her. Her lethal blow, however, didn't prevent the rat from landing his sharpened teeth into her forearm. Out of instinct, she shook the rodent's mouth from her flesh. Anger made her plunge the knife into the creature's stomach just to ensure his death.

She flipped on the flashlight and turned her arm toward the beam. Blood trickled out onto the white overalls. She could practically smell the rabies pathogen. *Looks like Stitch will have some work to do.* She reached into her pocket and pulled out the roll of med tape. All she could do was wrap the wound tight and hope Stitch had been exaggerating in her warnings.

Whisper resumed her focus on the sounds of the house. The battle, though brief and muffled, would have attracted the attention of anyone silently waiting for her to betray her location. Only the animal's death rattle encroached on the years-long melody of wind, sand, and insects.

Convinced she was alone, she turned back to her job as scavenger. There were still provisions to pilfer. When the Beast finally did roll its big wheels into town, there wouldn't be a lot of time to load up. Out of instinct as much as caution, she blended the sounds of her movements with those of the wind-driven sand as she stood and turned the flashlight on the room. Rows of dust-covered mason jars lined the shelves. From the solidity of their contents, she knew she had something worthy of the photosynthesizer. The wooden crates filled with shapely bottles also looked promising, though the black contents reminded her of the spittle from victims of the black death. After the early climate-driven famines, wars over resources, and inevitable diseases that followed, it was hard *not* to see death all around her. She stacked everything that looked potentially useful next to the closet door. Blade had been emphatic about the need to be watchful even when she thought she knew she was safe. Someone could always be creeping up on her. Advertising her position by moving the contents out of the room could be her undoing.

With everything set for the Beast's arrival, she again consulted her array of sounds. Other than the insects moving deeper into their wooden dens to avoid the noisy human, nothing had changed. Her hand hovered over the door handle. Hiding beat fighting, but if there wasn't any danger, curiosity won out over inaction. Just beyond the door was a room designed for entertainment and an entire house to explore. Someone from the past must have been a fan of music. With only a slight rasping of metal against metal, she turned the handle, letting the light of the room invade the pantry. So long as Whisper didn't amass a pile of stereo equipment, Swash couldn't deny her a few mementoes from her outing.

7

"*I*'ve got Blade on the com, Captain." Roach already had all six electric wheel motors engaged and waiting. They'd been sitting under the sand bluff for two hours—far too long for comfort, but with the static electricity generated from the wind-driven-sand, communications were dicey.

"What's his report?" Swash asked.

"With the growing sandstorm, his communication is only coming in bursts. He's got a legion of nomads on his tail, but from the tone of his voice, he's having too much fun to be in real danger. He sets our odds at four-to-one in favor of getting in and out unscathed."

"Have you noticed that whenever our fate is in his hands, his odds improve remarkably?" Stitch asked from the bridge's hatch.

Swash snickered. "When they don't pan out and we all

die, you can be the first to question his gambling prowess. What else did he say, Roach?"

"According to him, Whisper rated their find a four." Roach could practically feel Swash and Stitch's ears perk up. A four meant medicine, biomass for food generation, water —at least in some form—and maybe even some tradable goods, though Whisper had a strange way of deciding what was and wasn't desirable.

"That's good news for Blade," Stitch said. "I can't get that Iodine-X into him soon enough. Assuming we all get out of this mess."

Swash buckled into the navigator's chair. "I'm launching the hummingbird drones."

"Just please keep them out of the sandstorm. I still have two on my workbench I need to clean after that last outing with you on navigation." Roach liked and admired Swash, but the guy had no self-discipline when it came to working the equipment.

"Yeah, yeah, you just drive. At least I got mine back."

"Is there anything I can do?" Stitch asked.

For all of Stitch's many talents in keeping the crew alive and healthy, she wasn't worth a limp noodle when it came to facing danger. What Roach wanted was someone on the plasma cannon, but he doubted Stitch could take a life even if she did know how to operate the weapon.

Swash nodded to the alcove behind the bridge. "Get on Whisper's radio equipment. It's more powerful than our headsets. We need to keep an ear out for Blade in case he needs our help. I'd also like to get an update from Whisper on what she's found. I'm shooting the twin hummingbirds high enough to search for our weapons master. So long as he's got all of the marauders after him, we'll make a quick swoop to pick up Whisper and her cache then head straight for the jump spider. It'll probably get a little messy, but with Whisper back on navigation, I can man the cannon."

Driving without the benefit of the drone giving up-to-date information on the terrain ahead wasn't the best way to maneuver twenty-five tons of rolling habitation, but it beat having Swash barking directions. The Beast climbed out of its tire ruts like a sleepy drunk coming out of a cantina. The electronic engines were good for routine runs, but when it came to torque, Roach preferred the dual multifuel engines. With the plant oil running low and no go-juice, however, he kept his hand off the twin starter levers.

He caught a glimpse of the two drones as Swash shot them out of the front tube. Only when the holographic overlay showed up on the front display did he realize he'd forgotten to shut it off. He found it funny how quickly he'd become accustomed to the enhanced view screen. The Beast might not have been the best vehicle he'd ever piloted, but it was far from the worst. What really made the difference between staying or leaving was the way Swash took care of his equipment and crew. The man seemed to actually care. That was rare in a world based on every man for himself. Still, Roach knew his days on the Beast were numbered. Eventually, they'd all discover his secret, and he'd be driven off the roving platform and forced to find another way to survive. He needed to get across this fracking desert before he made a mistake. Hopefully, in the mountains he'd be able to live off the land until he found another ride.

"Are you paying attention?" Swash barked.

"Sorry, Captain. What did you say?"

Swash pointed to a pair of tire ruts in a nearby dune. "Blade skirted the town. Unless you want to maneuver this thing through city streets, I'd suggest you follow his lead."

That was stupid of me. His inattention not only risked getting them lost, but it also meant he might inadvertently use his enhanced skills. Even though Swash and Stitch were aware of his differences, if he let down his guard even once, he risked either Whisper or Blade noticing something odd.

Roach backed his foot away from the throttle lever and made a point of using his hand to adjust the handle. "Sorry, boss. Guess I'm not used to not having Whisper humming in my ear." His foot wasn't the only part of him he struggled to keep under control. The girl's innocence, understated beauty, and sense of adventure had been working like acid on his resolve to not divulge his secret to her.

Swash stood and leaned over the three-dimensional hologram displayed on his side of the dashboard. "Blade's headed toward the far cliffs. He'll have to circle back soon to avoid getting cut off. We'll have to move fast." He punched in a computation on the computer. "We should have fifteen, maybe twenty minutes at best. After that, Blade's going to run short on fuel. I'd just as soon not have to drive into a swarm of marauders to rescue him."

Roach turned the steering wheel toward a gap in the buildings. "Why couldn't they have picked a house a little closer to the outskirts?" Though the Beast could navigate within a normal city's restrictions, taking up most of two lanes made quick getaways nearly impossible.

"Stop whining," Swash said.

Whisper bolted out of the front door of a house, her arms loaded with glass jars. Roach shook his head. "How does she always know we're incoming? I could understand if I fired up the big engines, but I'm on electrics. This thing hardly makes a sound, and what noise it does make must be covered up by the storm."

Stitch was already handing out sacks as Roach brought the behemoth to a stop. "Medical first, then water and biomass. I swear, if I see one bottle of hooch before we're fully loaded, I'll use it to disinfect my lab."

WITH FOUR PEOPLE hustling the bounty from the house to the rover, someone was always on the Beast in case the unexpected happen. As with the others, each time Roach climbed into the living quarters after hauling in the groceries, he made a quick dart up to the bridge to check on Blade's progress. With the hummingbird drone at position overhead, if Blade was on his way back with company in tow, there should be enough time to get everyone back aboard.

"This is quite the haul, don't you think?" Whisper never seemed to be far behind him.

"You did good, kid." She wasn't much younger than him, but he used the term as much in affection as gentle ribbing.

"Thanks. I didn't have time to check the garage. There

might be something you could use out there. We're almost done with the provisions."

Roach couldn't resist the temptation to go snooping, though he wasn't sure if that was because the idea came from Whisper or because the prospect of raw materials for his machine shop was too good to turn away from. With Whisper still hustling her sack to the corner of the room and no one else watching, he took a leap off the railing of the metal-grate catwalk that circled the front and sides of the Beast. The ten-foot jump to the ground wasn't something a normal human would attempt simply for fun. Whisper had that effect on him—she made him reckless. He continued chastising himself all the way to the cinderblock garage.

With the exception of the layers of dust, the hundred-year-old cars in the relatively cool room looked like they'd been parked yesterday. Had it been another life, he'd have found the vehicles fascinating in an abhorrent kind of way. They were, after all, prime examples of what had kicked over the environmental laundry hamper.

In front of the antiques, he spotted something that made him run on all fours. "Guys," he yelled. "We've got water."

The half dozen glass jugs were just about the prettiest things he'd ever seen. Crystal clear, glass protected, and with the plastic seals intact, this would be the freshest water he'd ever experienced.

Swash dumped his sack as he ran into the garage. "Good going, Roach." He slung two of the jugs over his shoulders.

Stitch wasn't far behind. "I've heard about these but never seen one." She frowned at him but refrained from asking what he was doing outside of his assigned duty of hauling the supplies. She needed both hands to lift one of the bottles.

Whisper gave him a quick hug, which made him grow warm in the cheeks. "Look at you, being all hero-y." She fetched the next jug before retrieving the bag Swash had dropped.

As she sashayed behind Swash, Roach wondered if he'd just been played or if he'd honestly been the first to spot the jugs.

"Time to go," Swash yelled from the door of the Beast. "Blade's incoming, and from the closeness of the sand fleas on his tail, we're not going to have much time to load the jump spider."

Roach snatched up the remaining two bottles then ran to the Beast. Without breaking stride, he used his momentum to catapult the jugs up onto the catwalk and continued on to the back of the Beast. He pulled the launch bay handle, which swung the bay door up over the roof and extended the wheel jacks.

Blade tore around the corner, sending sand in every direction. The jump spider's engine sounded like it was choking from too long a run. Ten feet from the bay, he spun the vehicle around like a top and backed the wheelie speed demon to the rear of the Beast. When the back tires hit the loading springs, the jump spider flipped so that its front tires were up and its roof to the Beast. It was lifted back into position with Blade still inside.

Roach let go of the lever, dropping the protective shield back into place. The scream of pursuing all-terrain vehicles was instantly drowned out by the roar of the Beast's massive twin engines. Roach grasped the back-stair railing just as the six eight-foot-diameter wheels started kicking up sand. All he could focus on was getting back to the bridge. Swash was good behind the wheel, but he'd be no match for an attack force of marauders.

8

_____

*W*ith an enemy on their tail, Swash was grateful to have everyone back on board.

"They're herding us, Captain." From behind the wheel, where he belonged, Roach plowed the Beast through a sand dune that came up to the windshield.

"Noticed that, did ya?" Swash scanned the horizon. The mountain range in the distance was so perfectly framed by the display that it could have been a painting. "There's gotta be a freeway up ahead."

Freeway. Everything about the concept had become a cruel irony.

"Is that a bad thing?" Whisper asked from the navigation chair.

The marauders probably expected the whole crew to be equally naive. Swash knew better. "Not at night, but in the middle of the afternoon, the road temperature crests two hundred degrees. The river of black asphalt becomes nothing more than a sticky mess that grips at tires, melts rubber, and gums up the works. Hell, a person can't even walk across the roadway without having their shoes get stuck in the mess and catch fire."

Roach kept scanning the windshield display screen, which had the hummingbird drone's enhancements. "Hopefully, the semimolten tar and aggregate aren't covered by a layer of sand."

"If they're moving us south, maybe there's a way out north of here." Whisper always was looking for something positive in hopeless situations.

"Great," Blade said from the bridge doorway. "I'll keep my eyes open for a dune ten feet deep to keep our tires out of the soup."

Swash couldn't let the budding bickering distract him from their escape. "Whisper, pull out the maps and find me that damned freeway. Roach, get us ahead of these sand fleas, then angle north toward the open wasteland, but keep an eye on the mountain ranges. If you spot a gap in the hills, we're screwed." The only thing worse than running across a freeway was getting trapped in the corner of an interchange. "Blade, you'd better break out the plasma cannons. I'll join you on the stern mounts."

Roach took his eyes from the screen for a sudden check of the gauges. "One shot, and we lose a quarter mile of travel, Captain."

"I am aware," Swash snapped. Ever since he'd run a batt dry fighting off a band of marauders, each member of the crew felt it was his or her responsibility to remind him of the Beast's limitations and his own bent toward recklessness. "The more room you put between us and the thieves, the less likely I am to pull the trigger."

Roach adjusted the suspension's ground clearance, raising the Beast higher off the rock-covered ground. "I'll do my best not to lose you guys off the back. You'd better tell Blade to strap in. Looks like it's about to get a little bouncy."

"Right." Swash turned and ran out the door, crashed through the supplies still being organized by Stitch, and bolted through the rear side hatch. The hot wind-driven sand kicked up by the tires and lurching catwalk nearly knocked him over the railing. A bright staccato blast of machine-gun fire punctuated the light orange dust behind them.

"They're using projectile weapons, Swash." Blade never bothered much with titles, and even less so in battle.

Swash scurried to the cannon's harness then plugged his visor into the sights. The enhanced image couldn't do much about the disruptive sand that filled the air, but the outlines of pursuing vehicles and the deadening of muzzle blasts gave him clear targets to focus on. With his thumb on the dial, he adjusted the weapon to half power. Roach would appreciate the restraint. As the nearest asshole jumped his sand rail over a low dune, Swash pressed the trigger. He didn't need to see the scattering of lines on his visor to know he'd scored a direct hit. The fireworks of metal and sand cleared the cloud of dust behind them.

"Nice shot, Swash." Blade let loose a blast of energy from his cannon. Though his target didn't explode in a dramatic fashion, it did tumble into the path of two other pursuers. "Looks like gassers."

If the marauders were using petroleum, they'd have their fuel tanks slung low and toward the back. It wouldn't take much to blow up a sand rail loaded with gasoline. Swash dialed down the power on the lance and focused a narrow beam of electricity under his next victim. Instead of the impressive explosion, a line of fire erupted behind the stripped-down vehicle and lit up the other pursuers.

Even on his best days at the still, Swash couldn't produce a high enough alcohol content to leave a trail of fire like that. "They must have access to a plastics reprocessing plant. Fracking drill-hole holocausters."

"It's going to be tough to outrun them if they're driving gassers," Blade said.

That observation wasn't helping Swash think. Even if they did have some go-juice, the Beast was never meant for extended high-speed escapes. All he could do was hope there was some means of evasion. "What have you got for me, Whisper?"

"We're running parallel with the freeway." The girl's voice crackled over the headset. "A breakaway force is trying to outflank us. Whatever's ahead of us, they don't want us to reach it."

He considered directing her to fly the twin hummingbird drones farther ahead of the Beast, but Roach would be relying on the holographic map to keep them from crashing. "As soon as you figure it out, let me know."

Blade was already unhooking his plasma cannon from the railing. "I'll take the bow position."

Swash dialed up his weapon to full power. "Sorry, Roach, but saving our asses outweighs the need for distance." With one shot, he sent five sand rails crashing into each other in a fireball that lit up the attack force. Sand from a near miss by their pursuers pelted his arm. Projectile weapons and petroleum-fueled vehicles meant there had to be a marauder base nearby for supplies. Swash had survived a long time by skirting such encampments. "How far are we from the freeway?"

"About a mile," Roach said. "I've got it pretty well mapped out on the front display screen. From the glimpses of hot black in the sea of white sand, I'd say Whisper's map is pretty damn accurate."

"Any indication of a break somewhere?" During the wars, bombing roadways had been nearly as popular a tactic as sending false GPS readings. A deep unseen crater could swallow an attack vehicle whole if someone on the other side directed it over the edge.

"Sorry, boss. It's flat as pancake out there."

The *rat-a-tat-tat* of projectiles off the air scoop above Swash's head let him know someone out there was dialing in their range. Instead of ducking, he leaned into the plasma cannon's controls and scanned the approaching sand rails. Another blast of machine-gun fire betrayed the culprit. Swash let the ass biter have it right in the windshield. With the cannon on full power, the sand rail was cut in two as it sailed end over end. The explosion as the beam hit the tank sent the two halves smashing into its neighbors. Though impressive, the blast only managed to take out three pursuers.

"Persistent assholes."

"Aren't they just?" Blade's growling voice indicated he

was talking between clenched teeth. "I'm not going to be able to dissuade this forward contingent for much longer."

"Captain!" Whisper's usually restrained voice stung Swash's ear. "It's a bridge of some sort. The land falls away into a deep canyon to our left and a much wider bowl to our right."

"Describe the bridge." Swash lined up the cannon on the next marauder.

"It's solid concrete and rounded toward the bowl. Why? Does it matter?"

Swash let loose a barrage of fire at the good news. "Roach, head for that dam! It won't be paved. Blade, as soon as you've cut a clear path for Roach, get your ass back here with that gun. And Whisper, good going, girl."

From the display of hot exhaust plumes on the visor, it appeared the marauders were throwing it all on the line to stop their prize from getting away. Swash just had to hold them off long enough for Roach to get the Beast onto the narrow strip of roadway ahead of the attackers. With each bump under Swash's feet, he checked the ground to see if they'd made it to the roadway.

"Come on, Roach. Floor it, buddy."

"I'm doing my best, boss. I can see the incline. Hang onto something."

A loud blast from the attackers was followed by a hissing beside Swash. He let loose a stream of plasma into the crowd before checking over his shoulder. "They got the jump spider."

"That's why it's back there," Roach said. "Nothing's going to punch through to my multifuel engines."

Blade slid to a stop on the other side of the Beast's stern. He fired his cannon without bothering to load it into its mount. "It's going to be close."

Swash dialed his weapon back down to half power. With the marauders so close, he could see their blackened teeth on his visor's display. He didn't dare risk lighting up a petrol tank and having it explode, sending shrapnel into the Beast. He intentionally aimed wide of his next target. The shot sent the vehicle into a drastic turn toward the freeway of molten asphalt. Hot goo flew up from the large tires before they exploded. The sand rail flipped over, tossing its inhabitants onto the sticky surface.

"Not that I'm complaining, but what was that supposed to accomplish?" Blade asked.

"I wanted to send a little reminder in case any of those frackholes were thinking about outflanking us."

A hard jolt wrenched Swash's hands from the plasma cannon. Globs of black asphalt flew behind the Beast but only for a moment. With the Beast's tires on the solid, even concrete, the handles of the cannon settled back into Swash's hands. Before he could pull the trigger, Blade sent a stream of plasma right into the eyes of their nearest pursuer. The sand rail flipped over backward, taking the next in line with it as it sailed over the rim of the canyon.

Swash lined up on the next marauder but kept his finger off the trigger. "Once we're halfway across, aim for the dam. We're going to cut the roadway out from under them."

"They'll still be able to drop down into the lake bed." Blade never could accept a victory at face value.

"It'll take them a day at least to catch up. Right now, I'll take that advantage."

As the Beast rounded the middle of the dam, Swash lowered the sights of his cannon to below the roadbed. Marauders were still streaming across. Below the middle of the pack, he opened fire. Chunks of concrete fell down the cracked gray wall like a waterfall, quickly followed by tumbling trucks and sand rails.

Blade picked off the couple that had escaped the destruction.

"Which way, boss?" Roach's voice in the headset pulled Swash's attention away from their victory.

"Make a right at the end of the dam. I'd like to get as much space as possible between us and the marauder encampment before we have to shut down."

As the Beast rumbled to the other side and back off the roadway, the collapsing dam shook the ground.

9

With the bad guys sucking dust on the far side of the dam, Stitch lay in wait by the back hatch. She gave a curt nod to Swash then jabbed Blade in the shoulder as he grabbed the handrail to enter the Beast. "That should be enough Iodine-X to cure a four-hundred-rad exposure. Between the radiation and the treatment, you'll probably feel a little woozy for the next couple of days."

"Did you have to hit me like a fracking drill rig?" He rubbed his shoulder.

"If I hadn't, I'd be spending the rest of the day chasing you down." She turned from him and pushed her way onto the bridge. With Whisper still sitting at navigation, Stitch put a hand on the girl's shoulder. "I think it's time I had a look at that scratch."

Whisper pulled off the holographic headset and turned

toward Swash, who was standing in the bridge's doorway. "Can you spare me, Captain?"

He took her headset that allowed viewing of both birds individually. "Go. Get your booboo attended to, then get some rest. You've earned it. We all have."

Stitch kept her anxiety under control as she led Whisper off the bridge. Even under the bandage, it wasn't that hard to see the difference between a scratch and a puncture. The two red spots on the fabric meant it was a bite, and bites were a whole different problem than just needing a bandage. She ushered Whisper into the med-tech room at the back of the living quarters.

The girl sat at the medical desk while Stitch got her sample kit ready. "We both know that's not a scratch. What really happened?"

Whisper reached into the pant leg of the overalls and pulled out a plastic-wrapped bloody knife. "It was a rat. I thought you'd probably want a blood sample."

Frack. Hopefully, the feeling of danger didn't show on her face. Patients needed to be kept calm no matter the malady. "You should have come to me right away."

Whisper untied the knot at her wrist and worked loose the laces that ran to her shoulder before rolling up the sleeve of her medical coveralls. "We were a little busy."

Stitch started preparing her blood slides. She had no delusions regarding her position within the crew. Each person had a skill related to survival. Swash was in charge of making the hard decisions about what they were going to do; Roach maintained and drove the Beast to their next adventure; Blade provided security against the nomads; and

Whisper found their paths and scavenged what they needed. It took all four of them to escape danger. Stitch was the only one whose skills didn't translate to some activity beyond the Beast. She was support, and that meant her services invariably had to wait until whatever danger they were facing had passed. Still, without her, the crew might survive for a while, but it wouldn't be easy living—not that there was such a thing.

"Are you feeling anything out of the ordinary?" She drew a sample of blood downstream from the wound.

"You mean, am I foaming at the mouth? No. If it's rabies, so far it's not presenting symptoms."

"It wouldn't be this soon, but other viruses might." Stitch checked the rat sample under her electron microscope. The little bastard pathogens were practically trying to eat through the glass. She carefully set it on the desk, feeling like the rapid buggers were just itching to get at her. Next she examined the slide from the wound. The same rabies vector was present, but the microorganisms weren't moving very fast. She continued watching them, wondering if it was the exposure to the air that was dimming their lights. *Interesting.* Finally, she set the freshly drawn blood sample under the lens. The dead virus floated on the healthy blood cells like a defeated army. She moved the slide, searching for any still-kicking pathogens.

"How long are you going to look at that thing? Am I going to die or something?" Whisper asked.

Stitch looked up from the slide and realized she'd been so focused on examining the slide that she'd missed the girl's fidgeting. The big question was what to tell Whisper.

She opted for secrecy. The girl might not even realize her genetics. In the post-apocalypse world, not knowing one's personal ancestry was more the norm than the exception.

"I think you're going to be fine. I'm not seeing any danger markers. You might feel a little off for the next twenty-four hours. Don't let it worry you. If you feel anything more than nauseous, though, come and see me. Go get some rest, then check in with me when you wake up. I'll have your knife decontaminated by then."

Whisper gave a smile of relief that both warmed Stitch's heart and chilled her blood. Good news was always welcome, even if it hid a truth no one wanted to face. "Thanks, Stitch. I don't know what we'd do without you."

Once the girl had left the medical room, Stitch took what remained of the sample from Whisper's arm, added it to a culture disk, then dripped the rat's blood onto it from the knife. Whatever defense mechanism was in Whisper's blood hadn't given the rabies a chance to get established.

WHISPER HAD BEEN ITCHING to jump into her bunk from the moment she'd found the small flat computer screen in the girl's bedroom. Sending Roach after the water bottles had been a stroke of genius. It had given her just enough time to race upstairs and plunder the rooms. With the curved privacy door pulled down, she started ransacking her collection of cables. The device was old, perhaps old enough to have been used before every bit of data had been tethered to central control. If the long-dead girl hadn't bothered updating the software, there might still be something left on it. Otherwise, the hunk of metal and plastic would be just another piece of garbage that had been wiped clean when the internet went down for the final time.

Whisper found a white connection cable in the bottom of her bin that fit the hole at the bottom of the ruby-red case. Swash didn't like energy drains he couldn't identify, but he had to expect Whisper to be rummaging through her music collection if she was sick in her bunk. Everyone had distractions from reality.

"Come on, power up, my little friend. Tell me your secrets."

The screen was filled by the face of an overfed, hairy, slobbering dog that looked to be smiling. Across it was the white bar and flashing curser of a requested password.

She reached back into her box for the decipherer that Roach had built from her plans. "You think you can hide behind that electronic lock?" She giggled as she placed her universal key over the screen.

When all of the little icons showed up on the display, Whisper licked her lips. She lay back on her bunk and scrolled for the box with the musical note. Though no one would be able to hear outside of her compartment, she slipped on the headphones. She didn't wear them out of consideration for the others—she wanted to keep all of the music to herself. After tapping the first title to start her musical education, she went back to the main screen. According to the available-storage-space icon, the girl had filled three-quarters of the memory. Whisper could spend days or even weeks with the device before learning all of its secrets.

She opened the file marked Videos. A girl in her late teens laughed so close to the camera that Whisper could see straight down her throat. The image widened to show what amused her. A boy around the same age was trying to ride a board out in the bluest water Whisper had ever seen. A wave crashed over him, knocking him into the surf.

"I told you it was hard!" the girl yelled.

"Fuck you, Lindsey." The boy sloshed through the waves toward shore. He wore baggy shorts that looked so waterlogged they should have fallen off of his narrow hips. The sunlight glistened off the water like it was laughing along with the girl.

"So your name is Lindsey," Whisper said to the screen. "What a stupid name."

She flipped to the next movie. The same dog that had been on the first screen was jumping and barking like he didn't have a care in the world. The grass under his feet was greener, fuller, and shinier than any vegetation Whisper had ever seen. Trees stood around the field, but they weren't the wind-swept bare trunks she was used to. These were covered in leaves so dense she couldn't even make out the limbs.

"Stupid dog." She exited the videos and laid the device on her chest. Though the girl had been dead for a hundred years, she should have shown more humility for the environmental damage her generation had wrought.

She closed her eyes and focused on the song. "Stupid people. How could they be so oblivious to the destruction they were creating?" At least the musicians of the day understood suffering, even if it was only of the emotional variety.

BLADE'S SHOULDER stung like he'd been bitten by a radioactive fire ant. He thought he was about to cry, but it wasn't from the inoculation. He sat feet up in the parked jump spider, the one place on the whole craft where he could find some peace to be alone with his emotions. He turned the empty bottle of whiskey in his hand while reading the label: *Aged 20 years for smoothness.* He wondered what the original advertiser would have said about a bottle of one-hundred-year-old whiskey.

"Fracking greatest thing man has ever created, and I fracking poured it into the fuel tank. I am an abomination to humanity."

Sure, he'd been running out of go-juice. And the marauders would have taken more than just the bottle if they'd caught him. Maybe he didn't have a choice, but that didn't make the sting of losing the bottle's contents to the vehicle's engine any less bitter. He pulled out the now-meaningless cork and smelled the glass rim. The peaty smell of alcohol was barely more than a memory.

Blade wondered how Swash would have taken his thievery of the alcohol. It hadn't been the first time. The question of whether the captain looked the other way or was too naive to notice the pilferage didn't matter so long as

Blade was able to walk away from battle with something to show for it.

Running from the marauders had reminded him of the time he'd spent in their ranks. It wasn't such a bad lifestyle. Blade had been a hired gun available to the highest bidder. Though Swash didn't offer much, the Beast was the baddest rover Blade had ever encountered—and that was before he knew about the jump spider. He ran his hand along the roll cage. No one else on the crew seemed to realize that Roach was the real secret weapon. That dude could spin steel and aluminum into high-performance gold. Man, what the two of them could do together on the open road—stealing, raping, drinking, and gambling. The odds were so overwhelmingly positive that he considered walking straight to the bridge and hauling the kid out of the driver's seat. With no women to tie them down, they'd be kings of wherever they chose.

Not that Blade didn't enjoy women. Actually, he enjoyed them quite a lot, so long as he didn't have to get to know them too well. Women had an annoying habit of getting pregnant and slowing him down. He clinked the bottle to his head in an attempt to change the direction of his thoughts.

You couldn't have stopped what happened. Their deaths weren't your fault. That mantra had gotten him through a lot of sleepless nights.

He went back to admiring the bottle. Though he hated to admit it, he'd never have laid hands on it if it hadn't been for Stitch and her medical brew. There was a reason the house hadn't been ransacked in a hundred years. Disease was the marauder's true deterrent. Once, cops, courts, and incarceration would have discouraged thievery, but now the risk of death by disease took care of that.

"Okay, so maybe Roach and a med tech." Three was a good number, though not as good as two. With only two, he could steal the jump spider and be perfectly at home on the open road. Three would take some figuring. He looked around at the rails, wondering where a third seat could be added without screwing up the vehicle's versatility.

Then there was Whisper. The girl had been the first one to discover the cache of alcohol. The skinny, wily slip of a girl could get into spaces he couldn't. And best of all, she knew how to keep a secret.

The more he thought about going out on his own, the more he realized the only member of the crew who was truly not needed was Swash. Sure, he was a good captain. But in Blade's opinion, that just meant he kept his nose where it belonged—out of Blade's business. The biggest issue Blade had with Swash was his inability to choose profitable adventures. What they should have done was establish a defensible position inside the city. That place would have been a gold mine. No one just walked away from a gold mine. With a little negotiation with the marauders by Blade, they could have set up an honest-to-God outpost, making and selling food with the Beast's photosyntheziser, charging a king's ransom for fresh water, distilling go-juice and—though it went against Blade's alcoholic desires—maybe even selling the rare bottle of treasure.

He caressed the jump spider's steering wheel. That was

what they should have done, not gone off in search of some foolish girl's fantasy. Agreements were subject to change based on new information. Though it made sense at the time to go looking for Whisper's mother, it sure as blazes didn't now that they had the prospect of untold riches.

With his toe, he played with the jump spider's release. If only Swash had been a little quicker on the trigger, the sand rail would still be functional. Then he could have made a run for it, teamed up with the marauders, and figured out how to set up shop. Sure, the dam had been destroyed, but unlike the Beast, the jump spider could scale down the side of the empty reservoir, traverse the lake bed, and scramble up the other side. The worst case would be that he'd get radioactive mud caked into the tires, nothing that the shot of Iodine-X couldn't handle. The connecting hook didn't even budge, not that it mattered with the shot-up tire. Without clearance from the bridge, the latch would remain locked.

"Stupid thing's broken anyway." Blade pushed his thumb into the punctured tire. That was another problem Roach could solve with little more than the clothes on his back. That kid had no idea how prized his skills would be among the marauders.

Blade turned back to the bottle. "Such a waste." He tossed it over his shoulder to be left behind on the rapidly moving sand. After all, he did still have the other five bottles he'd taken from the house to console him.

10

*W*ith the crew snoozing in their bunks, Swash set the Beast's hand throttle to one-quarter speed for the night run. Holding the wheel spoke, he kicked his feet up onto the workstation-sized dashboard. Without anyone on navigation, all he could manage was one drone ahead and one behind, each on autopilot. A full holograph of the terrain was only possible by flying two parallel hummingbirds at a set distance apart, but that required more input than the old computer could handle on its own. The two-dimensional virtual map with the Beast at the center crept by under his feet on the combined dashboard and desk.

He needed to set up camp and put the supplies Whisper and Blade had scavenged to use soon, but he didn't dare risk shutting down so close to habitable land. As Blade had said, the raiders could still find their way across the dried reservoir, though Swash doubted they'd expend the fuel to continue their pursuit. But even though they'd outwitted that particular band of thieves, there were always more on the prowl.

The real problem was the lack of power and the need for repairs. He wouldn't rest easy until he'd put distance between his crew and the nearest available signs of human life before the limitations of the Beast forced him to stop. Thanks to their skirmish across the dam, they'd avoided the big cluster of intersecting lines on Whisper's faded map that indicated what had been a major city back when people relied on interconnected computer information. A lot had changed during the intervening two hundred years. There was simply no way of knowing who or what currently occupied the once-major city. The most likely answer was that it was where the marauders had set up camp.

He kicked the drawer fully closed. The girl's pilferage of the maps from the museum had been worth the effort, even if he couldn't allow her to bring the ton of books she'd wanted. He leaned back in the chair and only half watched the desert moseying by on the front view screen. The team had done well—better than he'd expected. As always, Roach had been his rock. They'd worked together long enough to know each other's secrets, including Swash's darkest moments.

He stared at the front view screen, imagining a very different terrain. The fifty-foot cliff overlooking the craggy shore of the north pacific had been an awe-inspiring sight, all the more so because Swash had intended on driving the Beast straight off the precipice.

"I didn't do it, did I? No. I don't think so." He looked back at the door, hoping no one was up to hear his outburst.

Everyone lost people, but few lost everyone at once. His former crew had been loyal, and that loyalty had ultimately gotten them all killed. He was still alive, and they weren't. That would haunt him until his dying day. It hadn't been self-control that had stopped him from plunging the Beast to its demise that day. If the crazy kid in the souped-up sand rail hadn't cut a path in front of the Beast, Swash felt certain he'd have hit the gas. Like having a bucket of cold water tossed over him, the shock had brought him out of his suicidal intention. Roach had saved Swash's life, though Swash hadn't admitted it to the guy and probably never would.

And Swash knew Roach's secrets at least well enough to know all the kid wanted was a sense of safety, and that meant staying on the move. The longer they remained in one place, the more likely others would see something strange about the guy.

Had it not been for Roach vouching for Whisper, Swash wouldn't have brought the girl on board as a member of the crew. Something about her had earned Roach's trust, and that was no small thing. Swash still worried about the wisp of a girl. She never wanted to talk about her past, which was fine by Swash but made figuring her out more difficult. His eyes drifted to the foot well in front of the navigator's chair. He'd caught the girl thief under there with her arms full of foodstuff Roach had stashed for his daily drive. Swash's first instinct was to drive her out of the rover at the end of a plasma blaster, but Roach stopped him. Whisper had been a slave to Scorch—a trader along the great lake that ran parallel to the Pacific Ocean—and had escaped. Accepting her meant the end of Swash's time plying his services along the West Coast—word traveled fast along the trading posts. But at the time, he'd had no idea of how hard the ugly man would take the human pilferage.

And then we were three. Three was a good number for the Beast—not so many that anyone ever felt crowded but enough that Swash wasn't constantly running from station to station. Though the Beast was designed to accommodate a crew of eight, he'd only once seen it at full capacity, and he'd spent his whole life aboard the roaming habitation.

He still remembered seeing his grandfather at the controls. The man hadn't even been a teenager when he'd signed up to fight in the Wars of Divergence. His stories were all Swash knew about recent history. Not that any of it mattered now. He caressed the steering wheel, imagining the old man's firm grip. The boy soldier had still been working his way up the ranks when the main government fell. In the chaos, Swash's grandfather had stolen what he thought would be his best chance at survival: the Beast.

Yeah, three had been a good number for the Beast, but as with anything good, others wanted a piece of the action. He didn't have a clear memory of how Stitch had come on board. He remembered contracting Sierra fever. That wasn't the sort of illness he was likely to forget. Outrunning a bunch of raiders, Swash and his crew had gone higher into the foothills than he'd intended. After one fracking little mosquito bite, he was once again facing death. The delirium had held him in its grip for days—there were still nights when he woke up in a cold sweat. He'd honestly thought he had died and was staring into the eyes of an angel when he was first introduced to the medic. She'd more than earned her keep on the rover by saving his life.

That day's adventure had been no different. Stitch's procedures had ensured that no one came down with the twenty-four-hour death, but it wasn't just her medical knowledge that he appreciated. She had a calming presence. Poking, tugging, sucking things out, and pumping things in weren't actions Swash was comfortable letting just anyone do to his body. On top of all of her other attributes, Stitch could cook. Having a team member devoted to keeping everyone safe, sane, and satiated in all bodily needs was a luxury he had quickly come to rely on.

Then there was Blade. Whereas three had been an easily manageable crew, four made them vulnerable. Swash had needed more firepower, but as the most recent addition to the crew, the ex-marauder was still an unknown. The hired gun might disappear at any moment in favor of a better-paying gig. But that day, he'd performed his tasks well enough, including bringing back the jump spider. That counted for something.

Swash stuck a caffeine stick in his mouth and chewed on the bitter end to keep himself awake. Nights traversing unending open space were the worst. Self-contemplation made him wonder why anyone chose to remain alive.

11

---

*S*wash was still at the controls when morning broke. Roach, ever the professional, came onto the bridge wearing his driving leathers. Most of the crew, Swash included, preferred to take a more casual approach to daily attire.

The guy leaned over Swash and checked the gauges. "You didn't engage the fuel engines?"

"I said I wouldn't."

"Yeah, but you lie."

Swash couldn't argue with the condemnation. "It was a quiet night. We've still got an eighth of a tank of fuel, enough to run the generator if we need to. From Whisper's maps and the drone coverage, I think we're a good hundred miles from anyone. What are your thoughts on setting up for the day? The batteries we have left are nearly dead."

Roach scanned the horizon. "I think we could all use the break. Stitch made a quick inventory of what we brought aboard. She thinks there might be some food that's still edible. The woody scrub brush out there might not be much use for the processors, but it'd make a decent fire. I could go with some freshly cooked food. Then I need to have a look at the jump spider and inventory repairs to the Beast."

Swash aimed the rover toward an escarpment. In the heat of battle, he never had time to assess damages, but once the firefight died down, he could remember damn near every bullet hole. "You'll probably need to check the back air intakes. There seemed to be a lot of projectiles flying around my head during the fight. Once Whisper's up, I'll have her fly the drone along that ridge. We might get lucky and find some shadowy valley where cactus can still survive."

Negotiating with Stitch for what biomass would go into vegetable-oil production for the engines and what for the food generator was always a challenge. As for making the precious go-juice, there never was enough sugar-rich material.

Roach smacked his lips. "You know how I feel about anything resembling tequila."

"Don't get your hopes up. Whisper will have to do some searching." At least being out of the area of blowing sand dunes made desert life a possibility. Even at quarter power, the electric engines started slowing. Swash worked the lever to no avail. The warning light glowed red, indicating that there was barely enough electricity for life support until the sun rose. "Looks like we've found our camping spot."

Roach patted Swash on the shoulder. "I'll set up the

extended solar array then start diagnosing what needs work while the batteries recharge."

Swash made sure all of the controls were shut down. "Give the jump spider highest priority. I know there's not much go-juice left on board, but if Whisper spots something other than plant life, we'll need Blade mobile to deal with the intruders. I'll come out to see what you've found after I put the others to work."

"Got it, boss."

SWASH ADJUSTED the soaking-wet cooling suit that covered him from ankles and wrists to neck before slipping into his leathers. The bodysuit made him feel clammy and gross, but at least he wouldn't overheat before the air conditioners came back on line. After changing, he hopped down from his bunk. At the back of the crew quarters, Stitch was busy preparing the photosynthesizer.

"How are we looking for food?" he asked. The chore that had once been his full-time obsession was one he had been happy to hand off to someone far more experienced, but that didn't mean he could ignore the basic requirement for life.

"Lots of spoiled can goods. They'll make fine substructures for the photosynthesizer. Only a few of them had burst open. The jars of homemade pickle soup are still safe to eat, though I don't know why anyone would want to. Whoever lived there had a hobby of filling decorative glass containers with different colored beans, rice, and pasta.

Fortunately, they sealed them all with wax, so the food didn't turn to dust. Oh, and there was this." She fished an oddly shaped plastic bottle out of the pile. As she angled it, the thick golden liquid inside crept up the side.

"What is it?" Swash asked.

Stitch seemed hypnotized by the goo. "Magic." She shook her head. "From what I learned about food, before everything went to hell, there was a specific species of insect that pollinated the majority of Earth's crops. Their demise was the first pebble of the environmental avalanche of terrors. As they became extinct, the agricultural world had to modify plants to be both male and female in order to continue their existence without the little flying cupids. If I'm right, this is bee honey. It's one of the few foods that can last practically forever. I'm actually a little afraid to open it."

"Looks like nearly dehydrated piss." History was for dreamers. "After checking in with the bridge, I'm headed out to see the damage. When the solar cells start generating power, get the food equipment up and running. I don't know how long we'll have here before someone zeroes in on us. I'm giving you a head start on that biomass at your feet, but once the still is functional, you'd better be ready for a fight. We need something for the engines."

She tossed him a drinking bottle. "Fresh water. You're going to need it out there. Just don't get too used to it. We'll be on reclaim as soon as I can get the recycler back on line."

He turned the scratched and dented bottle. Even under the age-whitened plastic, the fresh water sparkled in the light.

"You drink it, Swash, not admire its beauty. Savor it if

you like, but if there's any left in there when I come outside, I'll force it down your throat."

"Yes, ma'am." They'd been so busy staying alive that Swash hadn't considered what they had for trade. "Keep one of those jugs for us but stash the other five in the pantry locker. We may need them where we're headed."

He left Stitch to her booty and walked onto the bridge. Whisper was busy working the drone's controls, skimming the technobirds along the escarpment. Pockets of shadows dotted the display. Blade hovered over the hologram like a hawk seeking prey.

Swash took a swig of the water. It tingled down his throat in a physical manifestation of how it had sparkled in the light. "Take your time mapping the area. I'm not in the mood for surprises. I'll be outside setting up the equipment with Roach. Yell if you spot something."

Whisper nodded while Blade waved his hand at the outdoors without taking his eyes off the display and mumbled something indistinct. Swash opened the bridge's floor hatch and descended the short ladder to the desert. Under the Beast's fully extended solar array, the ground was pleasantly shaded, at least as pleasantly as was possible for air temperatures cresting one hundred thirty degrees.

The old Beast had saved Swash's ass yet again. He ran his hand along the lower armor. The MAZ-TIL-173-E had a wild combination of influences. According to his grandfather, the original design was ancient—part arctic explorer, part frontline command center, and all Eastern European paranoia. The vehicle's plans had been retrieved from history when Earth's environmental apocalypse became impossible to hide any longer. People needed to believe there was a way out, and many turned to nomadic living as a way of staying one step ahead of disaster. It must have made sense to the people in power that the military should follow suit. There was no way of knowing how many of the vehicles had been built.

As confirmation of the stories, all Swash had found was the brass manufacturer's plate in the driver's-side foot well. He and his father had turned the machine of war into something less militant, though some things, like the plasma cannons, made too much sense to lose in a world made up of thieves and murderers. Swash couldn't say life had gotten safer during his lifetime. That level of assessment would have required more information than what he could see firsthand.

He bent down next to the middle wheel while Roach hung onto the bottom supports like a lizard. "How are the batts?"

"The overlapping protective scale plates did their job. I'm not seeing any further damage to our undercarriage. If we don't go tearing through the desert like we did yesterday, we might get forty-eight hours out of a full charge."

With the unpredictable sandstorms lasting a week or longer, two days was painfully short. And their life support, locomotion, and weapons were all tied together into the only remaining useable cells, like three teenagers sticking their straws into the same frosty glass of agromalt. At any moment, one of them might feel the need to drain the glass dry.

"So power remains our number-one need. What other problems are we looking at?"

Roach rolled out from under the Beast. "Two of the six tires are damaged from running over the asphalt, but I have enough spare rubber to vulcanize them back into shape. They won't be pretty, but they'll work. The holes in the air dam's biofilter can be plugged. I leave you to deal with Stitch on that one. She's not going to be happy about reducing the crew quarters' airflow. Beyond those problems? Just my normal list of issues."

For a vehicle that was pushing one hundred seventy years of roaming North America, the Beast was holding up about as well as anyone could expect. At least the multifuel engines could still roar like great cats. At five hundred thousand miles, they were just reaching the prime of their lives.

Swash was grateful that Roach didn't recite the half dozen things he was short of for a full repair job, the most important of which was always their lack of time to do the jobs properly without resorting to the patch jobs that got them from one disaster to the next. "How's the jump spider?"

"They clipped her tire and shot up the skid plate," Roach said. "It shouldn't take me more than half an hour to fix. After we set up the fuel-processing equipment, I'll hop on the repairs." Roach was one of the rare crew members Swash never had to direct.

Swash led the way toward the rear lockers filled with mechanical equipment. "Now that we've got enough raw biological material to keep us alive and no one on our tail, what's your take on Whisper's request?"

Roach cleaned the sand off his agroleather pants while looking at the mountain range in the distance. "I've heard stories of secret military bases carved into the granite mountains."

Everyone had heard those fairy tales as children, but that didn't mean they couldn't also be true. Swash started handing parts to Roach. "Assume for a moment that the stories are accurate. Play it out for me."

"Like you haven't already considered every angle?" Roach laughed while setting up the equipment. "Okay. Working on the premise that Whisper actually heard a signal from her mother on that tinfoil contraption of hers, that would mean the old woman would have to have a satellite uplink. Since there's no centralized command that we know of, she'd have to be working alone or with a small paramilitary force. Every satellite hack I've ever heard of originated either from an old military base, some technology company's secret headquarters, or a whack-job nerd living under a rock. Those mountaintops would make a nice hiding spot for any of those options. Assuming it is military and her mother is part of it, we might be able to score some badly needed parts for the Beast. But even if that were true, we can't expect the woman to hold the door open for us. Just getting up there is going to be a challenge. Fantasy or not, the stories originated from remote locations. People with magical treasure like their privacy."

"At least I'm not the only one with reservations." Swash

was glad to hear Roach's words of caution. He hadn't wanted to be the first to speculate on what they might find.

Roach stared him in the eyes as he took the heavy extractor press. "Of course, heading up in elevation isn't just about climbing the mountains."

The memory of the month under Stitch's care still made Swash's skin itch. "We have a medic this time to tell us what we're facing. It's her job to make sure what happened to me doesn't happen to anyone else."

"Yeah, except Stitch needs the air decontaminators and their associated sampling units to develop her antidotes, and they have holes. I'm not saying we don't go, but it's not going to be a walk in the woods, boss."

"All in the search of a fairy tale." Swash didn't see much in the way of other options. Running parallel to the mountain range would just call forth more bands of marauders, and sticking to the middle of the desert would drain their supplies. "I sure hope Whisper finds some cactus. I'm going to need that drink."

12

Swash had his hands full resupplying the fuel tanks. The methane collector connected to the waste tank ran continuously, so that wasn't an issue. Setting up the high-capacity press for reducing oil-containing material to fuel the engine, however, involved borrowing equipment from both Roach's machine shop and Stitch's medical lab, and neither of them liked parting with their toys for very long. The collection of items sat out on the desert floor like the wares of a trading caravan.

After it was reduced to a woody waste product by Roach's hydraulic press, what remained of the oil-bearing organic matter needed to be fed into the enzyme extractor tanks. The little microbuggers could chew through a fifty-five-gallon drum of cellulose in an hour, thanks to Stitch's microorganism accelerator. Fully set up and shaded by the Beast's solar panels, the still looked like a small chemical plant.

The time spent processing the biological material kept Swash on edge. Though the Beast was a prize catch all on its own, it was the crew's life-sustaining equipment that the marauders were really after. They might have access to a gas refinery and ammunition dump, but the ability to make food and medicine required more than outdated equipment and forgotten storerooms. Specialists and tools had to work in harmony to support life.

Had it not been for Stitch and her equipment identifying the airborne vectors that covered the deserted town like an invisible cloud and providing a quickly distilled antidote, they wouldn't have been able to secure the bounty. He had no doubt that the deadly diseases were why the marauders kept their distance. Lying in wait until someone else did the dirty work was the thieves' primary mode of operation. Even if the assholes had stolen the rotting food, there wasn't a great deal they could do with it unless they had their own equipment. When he wasn't feeding the chugging, gurgling equipment that created fuel, all Swash could do was stand guard and wait. He trusted Blade to spot anyone lurking among the dunes, but nothing gave him more comfort than having a plasma blaster at the ready.

The driver's window over his head arced open, and Whisper stuck her head out. "I think I've got something, Captain."

Swash checked each piece of exposed equipment before heading inside.

"WHO'S GOING THIS TIME?" Whisper knew she sounded overly eager, but then, she had been the one to spot the small grove of succulents nestled in the shadowy canyon. That had to earn her a seat on the trip. "I know how to get there." Despite her attempt to control her excitement, the words seemed to gush out of her mouth.

Swash looked at the spread-out paper map and compared the hologram to the labeled topography. "Seems desolate enough. You're sure there was no activity in this junkyard past the ravine?"

Whisper looked at Blade, hoping he'd give a positive assessment.

"That area is beyond the drone's range," he said. "All I could make out was a wall of smashed cars. I can't imagine why anyone would be hanging out down there. Stitch's radiation reading was high enough to cook a maggot. Because the cacti are separated by the ridge, the levels are reasonable where we're heading."

"And you're sure you want to perform manual labor in this heat?" Swash asked her.

With him towering over her in the navigation seat, Whisper felt like a little girl with her father checking her homework. But she knew he was just looking out for her. "I can handle it."

Blade checked his blaster. "I guess I can keep watch."

"He went last time." Whisper wondered if she'd ever learn how to control her tongue.

"And you didn't?" Blade asked.

"Stop it, you two," Swash said. "I need Blade to stick close to the Beast. With all of the equipment exposed and running, we won't be able to hightail it out of here if danger rears its ugly head again."

"I can use the away time, boss," Roach said.

Roach was the guy who'd gotten Whisper on the Beast. She couldn't help her heart's increased beating each time she was with him. He was part big brother, part savior, and all mystery. She couldn't quite put a finger on her emotions for the guy.

"You built the jump spider," Swash said. "If you want to go, the driver's seat is yours. I want you both to carry plasma blasters. Even if the drones didn't detect anything, that doesn't mean there's no one out there. We should have just enough juice to charge the weapons' batteries. Don't get trigger-happy."

"I'd like to go, too, Captain, if there's room," said Stitch, who hardly ever left the Beast. "I can make sure what we find is safe to consume, in case you wanted it for more than just the engines."

Swash poked the spot on the view screen representing the Beast then the valley that Whisper had found. A squiggly line indicated the easiest route. "Five miles. I suppose that's close enough to rescue you if you get into trouble. You haven't been off the rover in months. Just make sure there's enough room to bring back plenty of fresh greens." He looked at Blade, who stood behind the rest. "Do you have a problem with my assignments?"

The big man shuffled a foot. "I suppose not."

"Good. Then you can watch the food-generation equipment while Stitch is away. It's not that complicated."

"The photosynthesizer is almost on line," Stitch said.

"I've already set up the equipment outside. Once the control light goes green, it's just a matter of adding biomass to the hopper. You can make sure nothing gets in there that you don't approve of."

"Can we go now?" asked Whisper, picking up on the tension between Blade and Swash. If things got ugly, Swash might change his mind.

Roach led the way past Blade, as if Whisper and Stitch needed a chaperone to pass the big man. "We'll be back as soon as we can, boss."

"No joyriding through the dunes," Swash said. "There's barely enough go-juice sopped up from the storage tanks to get you there and back."

THOUGH ALL THREE of them might have been able to squeeze into the two seats, Whisper hung onto the back rails behind Roach with her feet on the bar over the small engine. A fifty-five-gallon drum took up the space behind Stitch. In the cool suit, black agroleathers, and face shield, Whisper wasn't exactly enjoying the ride the way Lindsey had in the old electronic pictures of her in the dune buggy, but then, the girl clearly had never had a care in the world.

"Make a left at that ravine."

"You don't have to yell, Whisper. I can hear you over the com set," Roach said.

"Sorry." With the wind blowing on her, Whisper could just about imagine what it must have been like for Lindsey in her skimpy bikini, her hair being played with by the wind and the much gentler sun caressing her skin.

The more she thought about the girl, the more she hated her. Not for the first time, Whisper considered deleting all of the pictures. She really only wanted the music, anyway. But the images were all that was left to show the girl had ever existed. Even her bones would be dust by now. To destroy the final evidence seemed wrong. Not that keeping the electronic images was about honoring the dead—Whisper wanted to hold onto the last fiber of someone she could blame for the conditions of her life.

As they entered the ravine, Stitch grabbed Roach's arm and pointed toward the hills that separated the shadowy nooks from the expansive junkyard. "We need to take a look before we get too focused on collecting biomass."

Whisper leaned in, even though the com set would ensure she was heard. "There's nothing down there. It's just a bunch of crunched cars."

Roach slowly nodded at Stitch as if they were sharing a secret. "We'll check it out." He turned the big front tires toward the rock-strewn incline.

Sand was easy to brush off, but the orange dirt under the jump spider's tires sent up a cloud of dust that made Whisper's eyes burn. "You're sure this is safe?"

Stitch reached over her shoulder and patted Whisper's hand. "I didn't detect any radiation in the valley. We're far enough north to be clear of most of the blasts. Just say out of the wind."

Whisper had never paid much attention to the history of the battles that had ravaged the southern regions. She never saw the point. Beyond identifying the danger areas—which was mostly Stitch's job—knowing what had killed millions or people a hundred years before just didn't matter.

"If there's nothing to steal or obvious danger, why risk being seen?" Whisper asked.

"Humor me," Roach said. He seldom asked for anything from her, so that request betrayed his fascination with the pile of junk.

Whisper settled back into position. *Roach and his obsession with cars.*

13

_____

Roach powered the jump spider far enough up the incline to let him see the desert beyond the bluff but not so far as to be seen from the junkyard below the escarpment. It felt good to be back in the souped-up sand rail. The buggy had gotten him out of numerous tough situations and one that had been considered impossible to escape from—one that looked very much like the piles of crushed cars below the lip of the cliff.

He grabbed the overhead bar then slowed his pace. To catapult out of the steel cage might raise questions. When Whisper was off the back and stretching her body, Roach turned to Stitch. "You're sure about this?"

"If that area of debris is what we both expect it is, we need to know if anyone's left alive down there."

He didn't need to be reminded. "And if they've broken out?"

Stitch gave him a dismissive smile before glancing back

at Whisper. The girl was already looking antsy. "I just want to get a look."

With all three of them out of the vehicle, Roach checked his blaster. "Let me head up there first. I've had some experience sneaking up on places like this one. Follow along but keep to the shadows of the rocks."

"There's no one down there," Whisper said. "This is just a waste of time."

"Maybe." Roach concentrated on using only his feet and legs to climb to the top to avoid revealing his true nature. Behind a large bolder, he pulled off his com set and looked through his binoculars. "Frack."

Stitch hurried after him then pressed against the back of the large rock without peering at the settlement. She also removed her communication mask. "Is there anyone left alive?" She didn't sound the least bit surprised that the area wasn't the trash heap Whisper and Blade believed it to be on the hologram.

Roach dialed in the lenses for a better look. Hovels of corrugated sheet metal, twisted tree limbs, and dried mud bricks intermixed with more traditional desert dwellings. He could practically smell the stench from a mile away. "I don't see anyone." He made a sweep of the protective wall made of crushed cars. "They might have gotten out. I'd need a better look to be sure."

Whisper snuck out into the open with her binoculars. "What are you guys talking about?"

"Get down, girl," Stitch's controlled command carried a sense of urgency. "And take off that damn mask."

Whisper walked over to the rock as if she didn't have a

care in the world. She did, however, take off the com set. "What are you so freaked out about? Even if there were marauders down there, they couldn't see us way up here, and they certainly couldn't hear us."

Roach got down and scampered on all fours to the cliff edge. With his elbows in the dirt, he was able to better steady the high-powered binoculars. "I don't see any smoke that would indicate cooking fires. The whole place is pretty basic in terms of technology—no solar cells, photosynthesizers, or moisture collectors. It looks uninhabitable, but that's often the intention. They'd be waiting until some idiot marauder came in looking for easy pickings then jump the fool. I don't see any tire tracks on the road leading away from the mountain. Of course, that could just be due to the sands from the morning winds." He slid back to the boulder.

"If you two don't tell me what's going on," Whisper said, "I'm going to scream."

Roach slouched down the rock to a sitting position and looked at Stitch for guidance. The secret wasn't his alone. Whisper sat so close to him that their hips touched, or would have if he weren't wearing a puffed-up fake-body suit.

"It's time to tell her. It'll be easier coming from you. I'll keep watch." Stitch put the lenses to her eyes but remained close enough to the rock to be part of the conversation.

He looked at Whisper and nodded toward the ramshackle village. "Places like that one are called garbage-can cities. They were built to house mankind's failed attempt at self-evolution."

"I don't understand," Whisper said.

He looked at the sky. Not far beyond the canyon and opposing mountain was the Beast. He wondered if he'd ever see it again. But he'd known this moment was coming. Stitch was right—it was time Whisper understood.

"The first thing you have to understand is that when the prospect of human extinction turned into an accepted inevitability, things like medical oversight went out the window. The hope—or the insanity, as many scientists called it—was that freed of regulation, peer review, and contingency planning, fringe scientists might discover a way out of our fate. They discovered a way all right, but no one was quite sure what to do about the ramifications.

"They were called gen mods for *genetically modified humanoids*. DNA from embryos of species closest to *Homo sapiens* were spliced into the stem cells. The physically obvious attributes were designed to be recessive, not that it was supposed to matter. According to the scientists, the test subjects were sterile."

"Why would they do that? Humans are the most advanced species on the planet." Whisper sounded as sweet and naive as she looked.

"Their premise was simple. People used to breed animals, but every species we messed with became less able to survive. Take for example the noble wolf, which became the neurotic dog susceptible to every medical problem imaginable. Most of those canine species couldn't survive a day without human assistance. The scientific discipline responsible for what's over that ridge postulated that the same was true for people. We'd forgotten how to survive.

All they intended to trigger was a reboot of our basic animal instinct."

Stitch kept her eyes on the horizon. "Those test subjects were *supposed* to be sterile."

Roach let out a single grunt of disdain. "Here's the thing. Mankind really only excels at one activity: breeding. Take the most downtrodden, hopeless, and destitute culture on Earth, and they'll still bear children. Sex is like a free drug available to all to distract us from our situations. Even facing an overpopulation that sapped every resource and turned the world into a barren wasteland, people still managed to pop out more little fuckers."

"I think you're getting off track," Whisper said.

He shook his head. "Not really. You see, those gen mods might have been mostly sterile, but pull the trigger enough times, and eventually the biological gun will fire. When *they* started reproducing, normal people freaked. And here's another failing of twenty-first-century thinking: scientific specialization. The researchers honestly believed that by making their modifications recessive, even if nature did find a way to let them breed, their tampering wouldn't show up in the next generation. Like red hair or left-handedness, the oddities wouldn't count for much and would eventually fade away.

"What those eggheads fundamentally didn't understand was the sociological side of humanity. They ignored our ability to hate what we fear. If people could discriminate based on the color of a person's skin, imagine what would happen to someone exhibiting monkey characteristics. The lucky ones were merely segregated. The unlucky ones were hunted for sport. It shouldn't have come as a great surprise when gen mods gravitated toward other gen mods instead of mating with the general population as the scientists had expected. By the second generation, too many people realized the danger of a new species threatening the purity of *Homo sapiens*."

Stitch finally put down her binoculars, though she stared at the ground instead of at Roach or Whisper. "What was left of the government rounded up the gen mods for their own protection."

Roach wondered why Stitch insisted on defending the scientific and governmental actions. "Hauling off the gen mods only confirmed the rumors of alien-like creatures living among the general population. Anyone with long arms or ambidexterity was accused of having monkey DNA. Like the Salem witch trials, determining if a person was special often involved community testing rather than scientific analysis. After all, the modifications were supposed to be recessive, and since science was responsible for their existence, how was the general public supposed to trust their word? Of course, any dumb hick who thought his neighbor was a little too good at climbing trees could be counted as an expert in such things. Better safe than sorry. There were so many people rounded up that prisons wouldn't do the job. Unfortunately for the gen mods, the rapidly reducing human population provided more than enough abandoned cities. Then, like the witch trials, once the general population had dealt with the problem, everyone got back to their lives of denial. In less than a generation, most of these cities had been forgotten. Another advantage of controlling information and education—events that were uncomfortable were simply edited out of the human narrative."

Whisper's large eyes made Roach hurt deep inside. "You mean they just tossed gen mods into abandoned towns like that one to die of starvation and disease?"

"Is it really that hard to imagine? Human history is filled with stories of genocide. As for the walled cities, once the pumps ran dry, most gas-driven vehicles became items for museums. As if such institutions had a place in a dying society. Other than the occasional band of gasser marauders, petrol-driven vehicles are a thing of the past. Most cars were crushed into metal pancakes. There were so many of them they were used as mangled bricks to be stacked into walls around cities like the one over the ridge. Between the sharp steel and the embedded glass in the walls made of junk, not even a human hybrid would try scaling them. Due to the ring of metal surrounding the city, the inhabitants started calling those places garbage cans, and the gen mods were the refuse."

Stitch looked up from the sand. Her eyes glistened with unshed tears. "Those cities weren't completely uninhabited when the government took over. Not everyone could move to greener pastures. Between the contaminated water, lack of sanitation, and desperation, the once-bustling metropolises were already communities that humanity wanted to forget. The local inhabitants who stayed and survived were in pretty bad shape, genetically speaking. The original explanation given to the general population regarding the junked-car walls was that those places were for medical isolation. Only after the quarantine cities were sealed off did they admit that gen mods were a big part of the mix."

Roach leaned his head back against the boulder. "Like I said. People excel at breeding, and the genetically modified were like gods to the tumor-riddled masses. I suppose the original scientists were right about some things. Whatever natural evolutionary process had led to us being the apex species kicked into high gear, or maybe it was the radiation-induced mutations. Either way, instead of containing a new species destined to die out, each garbage-can city developed its own unique breed of monster. Or at least, that's how originals labeled them."

Whisper looked suspicious. "Were all gen mods based on the same monkey species?"

He laughed with derision. "Not all of them were even based on monkeys. Scientists first played around with their favorite species, *Rattus norvegicus domestica*—the common lab rat. Fortunately for the gen mods, even those eggheads were smart enough to realize that no one wanted rat boys, so they moved onto the next best thing—bats. I mean, who wouldn't want sonar hearing? Like the tails on monkeys, bat wings were edited out of the original DNA injections.

"Gen mods didn't cross over much during the first breeding cycles. I suppose there was some pheromone difference to distinguish the new species from each other. Monkey boys mated with monkey girls and bat dudes with bat dames. When the new humanoid subspecies did finally get around to getting it on, they were already consigned to the human trash heaps. Science was far away and long ago when the first truly visual hybrid emerged from the womb. The monsters that Blade said he ran into up north were likely bat-monkey humans further mutated by radiation. Due to the differing degrees of each species' genetic contribution, the area's nuclear contamination, and other environmental factors, each of those garbage can cities has developed its own unique brand of freak."

"So all of these gen mods are in these garbage-can cities, morphed into barely recognizable humanoids?" Whisper asked.

He wondered if she really was that naive. "Hardly. Give a prisoner enough time and no supervision, and they'll figure a way out. After that, like I said, people excel at breeding."

"How do you know so much about this stuff?" Whisper asked. "You're not some kind of gen-mod vigilante, are you?"

"Vigilante? No. I am a gen mod."

Stitch turned back to her surveillance. "You should show her. She needs to fully understand what you're dealing with."

He'd known it was going to come down to this eventually. "She'll freak out."

"I promise I won't." Whisper sat up and wrapped her arms around her knees.

He felt more than a little foolish standing up. "Don't worry, I've got a leotard under this thing."

Her blush made him experience a similar warming of his cheeks. He watched his hands undo the work overalls to avoid looking at her. The synthetic rubber body suit underneath his clothing looked real enough that he'd resorted to wearing underwear. He slipped out of the fake human body like a butterfly out of a chrysalis. With his elongated arms and legs freed from the fake body, he stretched them out from his relatively smaller torso. It felt good to extend his long fingerlike toes into the dirt. Though he'd grown used to having his body feel forever clammy, the breeze along his thin hairy arms and legs made him long for the days of swinging through the pine trees of home.

"You're glorious." Whisper stood in front of him. "Can I touch you?"

He held out his sinewy arm and turned it to show how much more flexible it was than her human equivalent. Her fingers tickled as she ran them through the short white-and-black hair. "What are you?"

"*Homo sapiens ateles.* My grandparents' genetic contributors were from long-dead spider monkeys. As they were an extinct species, the stored genetic material was fair game to the medical facility that concocted my ancestors. I suppose the doctors and researchers thought they were saving some part of life's diversity by using the old DNA."

"Did your grandparents look like you?" He could practically see the questions lining up in her brain, waiting for answers.

"No. Like I said, the changes weren't supposed to be noticeable. They looked human. The genes for physical appearance were as recessive as science could manage. Even my parents didn't exhibit much that would be considered unusual, unless of course you're talking to a paranoid society on the search for anything strange. They were tossed into the Tahoe garbage can as children."

She finally stopped petting his arm. "Is that where you grew up?"

"Yeah. The lake basin with its towering mountains was easily blocked off. There are only a handful of mountain passes, so filling the ravines with crushed cars was easier than surrounding an entire city. At one time, the area was quite beautiful. I can't say that's the case now." He didn't really like talking about where he'd come from.

"How did you get out?"

"The basin is quite big. There were a number of cities there before the ecology took a dump. Since the area was never all that accessible, physical books were more reliable than cellular signals even when it was inhabited by originals. Close off an area and deprive the inhabitants of outside communication, and they'll turn to whatever they can find. I spent most of my youth in the abandoned schools and libraries, studying the old writings."

"If you had all of that information at your fingertips, why did you choose to become a mechanic?" she asked.

"The high elevation made walking out of the basin nearly impossible. I knew if I was going to get out, it would have to be by vehicle, so I taught myself how to build the jump spider. Not much else to say really."

Whisper looked down at Stitch, who was still watching the desert. "And what's your story? How did you know about Roach? Are you also a gen mod?"

"No." She set the lenses down. "The mountain range wasn't the only barrier to the gen mods getting out. Being monkey based, a lot of them suffered from the same viruses as humans. Most who did manage to escape died of the same Sierra fever that nearly claimed Swash. Roach wasn't the first inhabitant of the basin to wander down from the mountains. I'd treated plenty of gen mods before he showed up. Showing kindness to the enemy isn't a way of maintaining any social credibility, and in the end, my clients were exclusively those living on the fringe—marauders, hired killers, and gen mods. I found Roach hiding in my infirmary, trying to steal medications. He was in pretty bad shape."

Whisper nodded. "So that's how Roach knew to find you when Swash got sick."

Roach slipped back into his bodysuit and overalls. "Now that you know my secret, you must see how dangerous it is if the information got out."

"Then why tell me?"

Roach caught Stitch's furrowed brow out of the corner of his eye, though he couldn't figure out what he had left out of the story that had her so nervous. "I've been around enough people to know when they're getting suspicious of my abilities. If we have a problem, I'd rather deal with it now than be forever looking over my shoulder."

Wide-eyed and openmouthed, Whisper looked like he'd just slapped her in the face. "Of course your secret is safe with me. I'd never tell."

He still wasn't sure if returning to the Beast was his safest play. Whatever passed as a community down on the desert floor would likely take him in, assuming there was someone left. He had skills that would be needed. "Swash already knows about my condition, though he's never asked about my history. I'm mostly worried about Blade. He doesn't come across as the accepting type."

"Swash would certainly choose you over Blade," Whisper said.

"Then what? The Beast still needs protection. Better to have someone we have some control over than start over trying to reform another marauder. Besides, turning Blade loose could end up with him telling fantastical stories in cantinas of his time on the Beast. Rumors were how my parents ended up in the basin to begin with."

Stitch got off the ground. "We're trusting you, Whisper. Having you know about Roach will make it easier to contain what Blade suspects. He listens to you. But you have to see that we're putting our lives in your hands."

ROACH POKED at the contents of the fifty-five-gallon drum with a stick. The cacti that struggled to survive in the shadows had developed long needles, making it hard to harvest their leaves. Inside the container, they looked like long-legged spiders with green bodies, trying to maintain their own space.

"I'm not even sure Swash can make anything out of this stuff. There can't be more than ten gallons of useful material in there."

Whisper had stayed unnervingly close to him throughout the gathering process. "I'd still say the excursion yielded more than expected."

He feared she might continue her innuendo-laced

comments when they returned to the Beast. "I need to know I can trust you, Whisper. If you can't control your comments, I'll head over the ridge, and you and Stitch can head back to the Beast alone."

She grabbed his arm. "Don't you dare. I'll be good. I promise. It was just a lot of information all at once."

"Well, get your head together. We need to start back soon, but I'm not returning until I know you can control yourself."

She stood a little straighter. He'd seen the stance before when things got serious. "You have my word." She headed back to the plant they'd been working on as Stitch dragged up her latest haul.

"What do you think?" he asked the medic.

"It's now three against one. If Swash is pushed into making a decision about who stays and who leaves, we're in a much better position."

Though Roach agreed that they needed the advantage, Whisper's belief that Swash would side with him no matter the numbers still warmed his heart. "So you don't agree with her that I was safe anyway?"

"You know Swash better than I do. My impression is, his primary motivation is survival. Having a gen mod and a medical collaborator on board makes him vulnerable. There are communities that would consider him a target for their fears."

Roach knew Stitch well. He wasn't sure if it was his genetic modifications or just baseless suspicion, but he could tell she was holding something back. "Do you trust the girl?"

"I like her. I know that's not the same thing as trust. We've both been burned by people we thought were friends. Dare I ask what your feeling are for her?"

Whoring around the fringe trading camps with Swash had been an experience Roach never hoped to have. Women were near-mythical creatures he dared not even touch, but Swash knew places where a guy like Roach, trapped in his isolation suit, wouldn't be questioned for his oddities. Now he had a woman who knew his secrets and saw him as more than an interesting science project. That made Whisper dangerous. He couldn't just walk away. She had already gotten under his fake skin before he'd revealed his secret.

"I don't know what to feel."

14

On the bridge, Stitch hovered around Swash like a mother hen. "You need sleep, Captain."

With every member of his crew back under the Beast's protective covering, he didn't have much to do other than pester those working the equipment. He made a check of the extended solar array's gauges to make sure every cell was functioning properly. "Why do you insist on calling me that when you're giving *me* orders? Seems like the title should involve the opposite power dynamic."

She snuck so close he could feel her body heat against his side. "Because it's the best way of gauging your level of irritation. When you're well rested, a little good-natured ribbing doesn't bother you. Sleep. I mean it."

"You go to sleep." He'd get plenty of rest if she'd just go to her bunk and leave him alone.

She slipped her hand into his. "I know there are demons lurking in the shadows of your subconscious. The others are going to be busy with the photosynthesizer and go-juice still for a good couple of hours, so they're not going to be looking to you for life-or-death decisions or me for medical triage. Come to the med bay. Let me help you. We could both use the rest."

He wasn't sure how him sacking out was going to help her, but clearly, Stitch wasn't going to let the issue go until he at least pretended to catch some Zs. He looked out the Beast's front view screen—no ground dust from marauders, no swirling white sandstorms, only the blazing heat of afternoon on the playa. The Beast was like a small bug in a vast solar-heated frying pan. Outside in their cooling suits, his crew was busy feeding the equipment. Stitch was right. There were more than enough hands working the equipment, and in his hazy mental state, he'd only be a hindrance. Still, he wasn't a fan of being poked and prodded in the middle of his sleep.

"Fine, but I can rest in my own bunk."

"*Rest* isn't going to cut it. You need sleep. But if you're more comfortable in your own bed, we can lie there."

He hadn't realized she intended on joining him. "You don't trust me to do as you command?"

"I'm the Beast's medic, and you're my patient. Like I said, I know you fear sleep. If you're uncomfortable with my prescribed treatment, I can give you a sedative, but that's only going to mask the problem."

"You know damn well I'll never take one." Losing consciousness to drugs was like being locked in hell. If he fell asleep on his own, at least he knew the door back to life was standing open.

"Then let me help you, Swash."

The sound of his name after her frontal assault of his title took the wind out of his sails. He got out of the command chair. With her hand still holding his, he felt like a little kid being taken to bed. "Stick a syringe in me while I'm sleeping, and I'll kick you off the crew. You can sit on the hot sand and watch us drive off. Do you understand me?"

She looked over her shoulder as she guided him back to the crew quarters. "Yes, Captain."

"And don't patronize me." He let her help him up to his bunk.

"Yes, Captain." While staring into his eyes, she unzipped the front of her jumpsuit.

"What are you doing?" Though the bunk was small, there was plenty of room in it for the two of them without shedding clothing.

She slipped out of the full-body overalls. "I've never been able to sleep in that thing. You might consider taking your sand gear off once in a while."

He felt foolish keeping the agroleathers on when she was out of hers. He unzipped his clothes and wiggled out of them while lying on the bed. Having the thick plant-based fabric on had always been the physical manifestation of his mental shield against getting too close to people.

Next went her cooling suit, and she was left in only her undergarment. The damp diaphanous white fabric did little to hide her naked body underneath. Stitch climbed in while he was still considering what to do about his own cooling suit.

Once she had the door to the bunk pulled down, she turned toward him. "We don't have to have sex if you don't want to. In my experience, the endorphin release helps calm the mind. It also results in an increased desire to continue living."

"Are you making a pass at me or prescribing a medical treatment?" Though he'd had plenty of women at the trading camps, he'd never slept with someone from his crew.

She bent her elbow and held her head with her hand. Her long brown hair fell out of the bun she usually kept it in. "Fulfilling sexual needs was a part of my medical education. A great number of problems—both mental and physical—result from extended abstinence."

"That didn't answer my question." He'd seen the drug-den whorehouses that passed as medical facilities. With a shortage of remedies, many people had grasped onto any form of relief they could find. Claiming something was medicinal expunged a number of sins. As far as he was concerned, he preferred his sex nonmedicinal and his drugs recreational.

She put her hand on his chest. "In order for me to be available to everyone on board, I have to maintain an aura of emotional neutrality. But that mental distance is never really possible. I don't offer sex to just anyone. *I* need the connection for the treatment to be of any benefit to my patient. But unlike mandating that you get some sleep, this is just an offer, not a demand."

He couldn't deny the physical response under his cool suit, and the prospect of his skin to hers made his eyes drift down her body. It was a small crew, though, and keeping them together required a captain who could control his urges. "Another time perhaps."

Stitch laid her head down on the crook of her arm. "Understood. Tell me what you think about when you lie in here."

Pressed so close, she didn't leave him much of an option other than to hold her hand. It was either that or lay it on her body. "I thought you wanted me to sleep."

She held his hand away from her breasts but close enough to make it clear the offer still stood. "I do, but focusing on drifting off is a good way of making sure it doesn't happen. Your mind must constantly be on the go, even though you won't discuss what's bothering you. Just talk to me about anything. How did you end up with the Beast?"

Women had such weird ideas about light conversation. "She belonged to my grandfather. He served during the wars."

"I've never heard a good explanation of that time in history. What did he tell you?"

Swash hoped regurgitating what he knew of the past wouldn't result in his usual barrage of nightmares. He'd seen the images enough times in his imagination that it was like he'd lived through every stage of man's destruction. "People had such simplistic ways of thinking. Climate collapse, nuclear obliteration, pestilence—no one thought to tick the box labeled 'all of the above,' but of course, it was. One disaster naturally fell into the next like dominoes toppling. Once the weather became too unpredictable to support agriculture and the results no longer able to be hidden, people resorted to their naturally aggressive habits. Since life was already teetering on the edge, they didn't see a reason to hold back on the weapons they used."

She held his hand with both of hers like it was a security blanket. "I'm very familiar with the nuclear fallout and the physical deformities that rippled into future generations."

He was pretty sure he didn't want to add her monsters to his nightmares. "Like cockroaches crawling out of the rubble, people found a way to survive. Those that didn't die thought they'd dodged the worst of it. They were wrong. The dead passed diseases to the living."

She nodded. "Without the higher life forms to keep the buggers in check, insect-carrying pathogens ran amok."

"For many, the suffering became too much. Suicide. The word moved from a mental condition to a full-on obsession." He remembered the effects that plagued one person after another, right down to his mother. "Movements were formed around the idea of mankind being the ultimate form of cancer, and the most reasonable answer was to become part of the *self-limiting*. The term used to refer to sicknesses that eventually ran out of steam and died off. Mankind could do the same, except with intention."

Stitch snuggled her leg against his without making a comment.

"By the time the dusts of destruction had settled, less than ten percent of the human population remained. Most considered that number better than expected, but of course, those people were the ones who'd survived." Swash suspected the dead might have a less optimistic interpretation of the results. "What the numbers failed to convey was the damage done to human history and intellect. Science was blamed. Industry was vilified. The greatest creations of human existence were seen as abominations against life on Earth. Knowledge—the single greatest attribute of the human species—was viewed with derision."

She squirmed closer, rolled him onto his back, and rested her head on his chest. "But we're still here."

She was right. Against all odds, he was still alive. His mother had succumbed to the religion of death. If it hadn't been for his father whisking him away in the Beast, she might have taken Swash into the afterlife with her. It wasn't as if he had much of a future to look forward to.

If only his father and grandfather hadn't given Swash the benefit of their vast experiences and educations, he might find sleep easier to tolerate. Knowing what had happened made it hard to drift off, and even if he could shut off the thoughts, unconsciousness was the realm of nightmares. He snuggled against Stitch, hoping she had fallen asleep without noticing that he was still awake.

15

Back behind the Beast's controls, Swash wasn't sure how much sleep he'd gotten. Having a nearly naked woman next to him had proven to be remarkably relaxing, far more so than he'd expected. The fact that sexual encounters were among Stitch's services wasn't surprising. He wasn't sure why he hadn't taken her up on the offer. Maybe because, like suicide, the longer he put off having sex with a member of his crew, the better he felt about himself. Despite the matter-of-fact way she'd offered the treatment, he didn't intend to share the information with the rest of the crew. Doctor-patient confidentiality seemed like the kind of trust that should work in both directions.

At the navigation station, Stitch fiddled around with the drone's controls like she was confused about something. He was only slightly worried she was about to lay into him in front of everyone about him not having sex with her. "Out with it. What's bugging you?"

She pointed at the layered sandstorm. "Before we climbed the ridge, I took some readings of the junkyard beyond the canyon. The radiation wasn't good but not as bad as I'd told Blade. I wanted to keep him off of the away team. I didn't think anything of the readings at the time. The great nuclear trench is somewhere south of us, so there was bound to be some radiation. Being in the box canyon shielded us from the radioactive wind, and as the Beast is in the wind shadow of the low-lying hills, I figured we were safe."

"You're saying we're not?" Swash wondered how difficult it would be to decontaminate the food provisions they'd made in the last twenty-four hours.

"No, we're safe from any nuclear fallout. That's what worries me. I'm not picking up any radiation from the storm. There must be another low mountain range between us and the trench."

Swash didn't like mysteries. Whenever possible, he would fire up the Beast's engines at the first sign of inconsistency. "And that storm is just the kind of disturbance an enemy might use to hide their approach. You're sure you didn't see anyone on the valley floor?"

She looked at Roach standing behind her as if they were sharing a secret. The kid turned toward the window. Outside, Blade was working on the photosynthesizer.

Roach turned to Swash. "It was a garbage-can city, boss. I didn't see anyone down there, but we didn't do a full reconnaissance. There were enough indications of life to make me worry."

Swash nodded. The gen mods were a secretive bunch, and with good reason. Entering one of their enclaves was a dicey proposition. Strangers could be met with offers of trade or just as easily have their throats slit. And trading-post horror stories described them swooping out of a sandstorm like wraiths to take what they wanted. "It was too far away for the drones even before the winds picked up, so we've got no way of being sure it was deserted."

"I could outfit and launch the magpie," Whisper said from her communications center outside the bridge. "It has more power than the hummingbirds. It still won't reach the city, but at least we'll see if someone's sneaking up on us."

"Do it, but don't send it past where you guys were scavenging. If someone is down there, I don't want them to know we're still here. Go straight there and straight back. While you're doing that, Roach, Stitch, and I will help Blade break down the equipment. I think we've lingered here about as long as we dare."

Though setting up the equipment up took time, in an emergency, it could be taken down in a less than half an hour. If Whisper spotted someone, Swash was prepared to cut that time in half.

SWASH PULLED the rear hatch closed against the growing sandstorm. All that remained of the campsite were footprints in the sand and indentations from the equipment, which the wind would soon wipe clean. He slipped between the barrels of unprocessed biomass and partially fermented go-juice. In the bridge, Blade replayed the hologram while Whisper brought the drone home.

"What have we got?"

Blade zoomed in on the humanoids swarming the canyon. "The monsters squatting in that old village are aping it up in the ravine. Guess they didn't like having their cactus garden raided."

Swash took the pilot chair. Though Roach was a better driver, he didn't want to force the kid into making life-or-death decisions for the crew if they ran into problems.

"Which way are we headed?" Blade hovered around the bridge like a kid waiting for his Christmas presents. The guy's lust for battle sickened Swash.

None of the options were appealing. Going back the way they'd come meant running across the marauders. And if word had worked its way to Scorch about where Swash had headed, the area could already be set with ambushes. Striking out over the ridge meant dealing with the residents of the garbage-can city who were taking refuge from the storm in the canyon. Hunkering down with them would likely lead to a fight.

His only remaining option sent a shiver down his back. "I'm taking her into the storm. Whisper, you'll want to lower your antennas. Roach, close the solar cover over the roof. Stitch, you'd better seal up the rear scoops and put the air on recirculation. Blade, batten down anything you find. It's going to get ugly out there."

With everyone rushing to their stations, Roach took the

navigator's chair and activated the external shields. "Are you sure about this, boss? Those storms can outlast our batteries."

Swash fired up the multifuel engines and put the rover in gear. "We've got a better chance of outrunning the storm than staying put and waiting it out. Eventually, those winds will coat the whole area in dust and sand. I don't fancy being buried in a drift. Thanks to our day of production, we've got enough plant oil to take us across the desert." He looked over at Roach while checking to make sure they were alone. "I'm sorry about Blade."

"No need to be." Roach checked the overhead light panel that indicated any open hatch. "I've heard worse insults than *ape* and *monster* in my time."

As the Beast rounded the outcropping of rock, the nose lurched to the side from the force of the wind. With no drone mapping out what was ahead and only vague shapes in the umber-hued view screen, Swash set the throttle to foot control. The old-fashioned way of driving meant utilizing every limb to stay in the driver's seat while combating the elements, but he didn't dare risk taking them over the lip of a canyon while fumbling for the hand lever.

"You've done this before, right, boss?" Roach braced himself against the side of the cab.

Swash took the old metal steering wheel with both hands. Even with the power assists designed to combat nature's influence, the storm made itself felt through every control. "My grandfather once pedaled this rig through a category five hurricane. The water level came clear up to the view screen. Waves were sloshing over the top. I was certain we were going to drown. I must have been about five years old at the time."

"What happened?"

Swash chuckled. "The old man starting humming loud enough to be heard over the storm. It was like he was putting it in its place. She could howl and batter and send lesser vehicles flying through the air, but to my grandfather, she was still only a mild annoyance." Swash leaned hard into the side of the chair as the wheel tried to flip him out of it.

"He sounds even crazier than you. I didn't think that was possible."

Swash stared down at the transmission controls, wishing he had another hand, though if he did, he'd have that, too, on the wheel. "Put yourself to some use. The wind's battering me hard. I need more torque on the starboard engine if we're going to swing her into the wind."

Roach grabbed the dashboard support rail and crabbed his way from the navigator's chair to Swash's side. With his feet spread wider than a normal human would find comfortable, he took one hand off the steel bar and grabbed the power lever. "How do you want the gears?"

Even with the steering wheel turned a quarter turn to the left, the Beast was still clawing to the right from the wind. "Set them both to double-compound low, then put the engine-torque settings on individual manual control. I want to keep the wheels from spinning through the sand."

Though the wind and sand still dominated the acoustics as they beat on the metal sides, the mammoth engines at the back of the Beast roared like angry dragons coming out of their den. The three wheels on the starboard side bit hard into the loose sand, sending up a swirl of white and ocher into the downwind section of the storm. In the view screen, the bombardment of tiny grains shifted from across the field to straight on.

"You're not taking me down," Swash growled.

When the Beast was lined up directly into the onslaught, Roach adjusted the levers until the two engines were matched in their assault against the desert floor. "If you've got a guess on which direction we're headed, I can pull out Whisper's maps."

"Even if I did, I couldn't tell you if we're moving forward or being shoved back by the wind. My primary objective is to stay aboveground."

Roach leaned over the dashboard and peered down at the angled section of display screen. "The tires aren't bogging down, so I'd say we're headed forward. We must be past that garbage-can city by now. I'd really like to get a look at those maps. We don't need to drive over a freeway in this mess. Think you can spare me for a second?"

"Do it. Just don't send those pages flying. I'm having a hard enough time seeing as it is. If the wind shifts off my nose, get your hands back on those levers."

So long as he kept the wind straight to the bow, steering wasn't half the issue it had been earlier, but that didn't alleviate Swash's tension. If he laid into the accelerator too much, the wheels might dig the rig straight down to hell before he realized it. Too little, and the wind might have its way with the Beast, sending it flying end over end.

Roach spread out a map on the dashboard. "I don't see anything north of that village for a hundred miles. Doesn't even look like they bothered listing the roads, if there were any." Even though the kid was yelling, Swash still had trouble hearing him.

Seeing where they were going was the least of Swash's worries. Though his weight couldn't possibly make any difference relative to the twenty-five tons of moving metal, as the wind lifted the nose of the Beast, he leaned over the wheel. He wanted to scream at the storm, but giving in to anger wasn't the way he'd been taught to drive.

"This little light of mine, I'm gonna let it shine," Swash sang.

Roach joined in for the second line. "This little light of mine, I'm gonna let it shine."

Swash couldn't tell if Roach thought his captain had lost his mind and was just humoring him or was joining him in his insanity. The kid dropped the map and grabbed both engine levers, and as they sang louder, he pushed the handles closer to the view screen. At maximum torque, the vehicle wouldn't be setting any speed records, but the storm would have to do more than just pummel the Beast to get her to submit. The rumbling engines provided a deep base note to their singing.

"What the hell is going on up here?" From the racket behind Swash, it sounded like Stitch had careened through the hatch and was bouncing from wall to wall.

The Beast rocked from side to side, though Swash couldn't decide if that was a nod to Stitch or an attempt to make her return to her seat. "Just trying to lighten the mood. How are things in the crew quarters?" he screamed, maybe to be heard over the wind or maybe as another sign of his growing insanity.

"Blade threw up his lunch," Stitch said. "Even strapped into her chair, Whisper has found a way to huddle into a ball. Being under the command of two lunatics isn't helping with morale."

"Is that your professional diagnosis?" Roach jockeyed the power levers in response to the changing wind conditions.

Swash tried to remain sane, though he wasn't sure what that meant in regard to carrying on a conversation while fighting for everyone's lives. "It would be best if you returned to your seat and strapped in."

Stitch lunged forward, reached out with both hands, and grabbed the dashboard handrail. Then she pulled herself upright. "I can't see how you two are managing to control this monster, but you're going to need food and water if you intend to keep at it. I've got some in my coat pockets, but I don't dare let go of this handle."

Roach lifted his foot and sent his shoe flying against the back bulkhead. With his long flexible toes free, he reached into her pockets for the provisions and deposited them in the storage slot next to Swash. "You might want to close the bridge door on your way out."

As she nodded, her hair fell over her face. Though the thought was completely illogical and out of place, Swash envisioned her in his berth, barely clothed and pressed against him. "Thanks for the grub."

∼

SWASH DIDN'T REMEMBER when the wind had died down or how he'd pulled the Beast to a stop. His hands were still gripping the wheel when he lifted his head off of the support bars. Since he was facing the navigator's chair anyway, he attempted to focus on Roach. With his clothing and body suit torn, his spindly arms and legs glistened with the sweat of his wiry hair.

"You still with me?" The words rasped against Swash's throat.

Roach pulled his arms under his head on the navigation station and pushed himself up. "I think so. Anything broken?"

Swash was slowly regaining feeling in all four limbs. "On me or the Beast?" He turned to look out the view screen. A field of sand spread out before his eyes.

Roach fell back into the chair. "You. We've got a lot of work to do before we can figure out our vehicle's condition."

Swash didn't want to get out of the chair, but his body was registering aches and pains from head to toe. Standing was his only way of shaking things out. With his hands on the support handle beside the pilot chair, he yanked himself upright. "I seem to be functional. I'll check on the others. Soon as you're able, start running diagnostics. We've got a long day ahead of us."

"Right, boss."

Swash tried to take a step and ended up falling into the bulkhead. "Sons of the rich. I may not be in as good a shape as I thought. Damn left leg is locked up hard as a steel beam."

Roach worked his way off the chair. From his stretching, it was clear he'd faired far better than Swash. "You want me to get Stitch?"

Swash shook his head. "We can't risk you giving away your secret. I'll be fine. Just give me a minute."

Roach looked down at his body as if not realizing what he'd been through. "Stitch has a spare body suit for me. We thought it'd be safer hiding it in the med bay than among my things."

Swash hobbled to the hatch. After making sure Roach wouldn't be seen, he opened the door and pushed his way into the living quarters. The floor was strewn with the contents of berths, storage cabinets, and stomachs.

Though the Beast was pitched at an inconvenient angle, Whisper worked the small stove. "I thought you could use some of Stitch's coffee after a day of chewing caffeine sticks."

He took the hot mug in both hands as if it were liquid life. "How did you fare?"

"A little bumped and bruised but nothing that required treatment. Blade's in medical with Stitch. He dislocated an arm when the Beast went onto its side."

Swash had to think back through the nightmare of images. The front left tire had hit something, driving the starboard side down hard. Roach acted like a madman furiously working the power levers while Swash had turned the wheel farther than it should have gone. "I guess I need to add a broken front axle to Roach's list of repairs."

"How did we get back upright?"

Swash shook his head. "Roach was all over the dash,

switching gears, throwing levers, and God knows what else. I think he opened the solar roof panels' protective shield. The wind caught it like a sail and set us back on our tires. It's all kind of a blur." He sipped the hot coffee.

"Any idea where we are?" Whisper asked.

Location was only really relevant in terms of danger or destination. They hadn't been descended on by marauders, which meant they were okay for the moment. As for the Rocky Mountains, they wouldn't know much until they could get the doors open. "We're still in the desert."

"I figured that much."

His hip was telling him he needed to get off his feet. "When Stitch is done with Blade, tell her Roach needs some private body repair. I need to lie down."

"What should I tell Blade?"

Swash wondered if the big dude would listen to anything a woman told him to do. "We need to see the outside of the Beast. He can start working on freeing the side hatch of sand. Oh, and when Stitch is done with Roach, have her knock on my berth."

"I figured that was a given from the way you're limping, but I'll make sure Roach's secret is safe before she turns her attention to you."

16

Swash still felt like hell, but at least with his leg immobilized, medication flowing through his veins, and coffee warming his stomach, he could function. With Stitch's help, he made it out of the cantilevered side hatch. The morning sun baked the white sand. The new dunes looked like frozen wave crests stretched out on a great dry ocean.

"You want the bad news first?" Roach asked from the catwalk that was even with the top of the dune.

"I assume that means there isn't any good news?"

Roach held up his hand and grabbed a finger. "Busted front axle, missing solar shield, one solar panel heavily damaged, and another one I think I can repair. And that's just from what I can see so far."

"How about our running gear?"

"The engines are fine. I swear, you could point the Beast in any direction, and those workhorses would power her around the world without ever turning the steering wheel. I haven't been able to get to the batteries, but the gauges read okay. I'm a little concerned about the tires. At full torque, we were stressing the airless rubber lattice pretty hard. Blade's working on clearing away enough sand so I can access the exterior storage lockers. We should have her free of this sand dune by dark."

"As soon as we get the axle fixed, I want to get moving. I've already had about enough of this desert."

"I hear ya, boss. Blade says he'd like permission to take out the jump spider."

Swash wasn't surprised, though he thought it unlikely that there would be a threat. As an ex-marauder, sometimes the guy just needed time to himself. "I'll talk to him."

Roach looked at Stitch then back at Swash. "I think he might be a little inebriated."

Swash balled his fist. A little pilfering once in a while was one thing, but Blade's thievery was getting out of hand. And showing off the results was unacceptable. As Swash turned toward the back of the catwalk, Stitch put her shoulder under his arm.

"What are you doing," he asked.

"Shut up and let me help you. Until I can get you off that leg, you're going to have me attached at the hip. Plus, I don't think you really want to confront Blade alone while neither of you are at your best."

As she helped him along the side of the Beast, he feared she might be right about him needing her help. His partially immobilized leg hit every obstacle in his path. With the Beast half-buried, however, getting onto the desert floor didn't require the use of the ladder. The old girl looked like a locomotive that had run off the rails. During the storm, a dune had built up along one side of the wreck. Swash had seen his beloved rover in worse condition but not recently.

He tapped his com. "Roach, think you can stabilize that busted axle? Shoveling the sand is going to take longer than expected. I think we're going to have to drive her out."

"If I can get out of the bridge's floor hatch, there might be a pocket of air under us. It'll still take some digging to get to the axle. I'm not crazy about the idea of being buried, though." Roach's grumbling made him sound as tired as Swash felt. Working under the Beast while she was stuck in the earth was never ideal.

"Take a look and let me know what you need." Swash switched off the com. The conversation with Blade wasn't going to be one the rest of the crew needed to hear.

The big man leaned on a shovel near the back tire. Only a sliver of the metal-and-rubber-composite tread showed over the sea of white. "She's stuck good." The slight indentation around the rig indicated that Blade hadn't been putting his all into the digging.

"I've got Roach working on something quicker than digging. What's your tactical assessment of our situation?"

Blade looked around at the ridges of sand. "Hard to say without knowing where we are, but that storm would have buried a lesser vehicle. Have you launched the drones yet?"

"I wanted to hear from you first. If there's a band of marauders camouflaged in the vicinity, I'd rather not announce where we are. Roach says you want to take the jump spider out for a reconnaissance."

Blade nodded toward the rear of the Beast, where the dune angled steeply. Getting the sand rail out wouldn't be easy. "She's still mostly buried, but if we could lift the shield, I think I could power her out. It'd make me feel a lot less jumpy if I knew we were alone out here."

Swash listened as much to the big man's tone as to his words. Marauders had sneaky ways of outwitting sandstorms, but even a reformed pillager wasn't likely to share his secrets. Since Blade sounded nervous and slightly slurred, Swash had to assume the threat was real. Firing up the Beast's engines and sending sand flying in all directions would be far more noticeable than flying a drone. Sending out the jump spider, however, might distract anyone looking for the bigger prize.

"Round up what you need and get behind the wheel. I'll lift the shield out of your way. And keep your com on. As soon as Roach has the axle immobilized, I want you off of the sand. You're not going to have all day to dune hop."

"Swash," Stitch said. He assumed her hand against his stomach was meant to remind him about Blade's inebriated condition.

"Right." He hated reprimanding anyone. "Word is, you've got some hooch stashed on board. I'd rather not have to search you each time you return from a raid, but we need every provision you scavenge. You're still new enough on my crew to be given the benefit of the doubt, but don't delude yourself into thinking I wasn't aware of what you were doing. Turn over half of what you stole, and we'll call it square. In the future, though, steal from me, and you're off my rig."

Blade straightened up as if preparing for a fight. "I didn't steal anything. I considered it payment for services rendered. Still do. I'm not part of your merry crew. I'm a gun for hire. In the absence of payment, I'll collect what I'm owed in any manner I see fit. So I'm keeping the bottles."

Every roving community had its own rules, and when it came to the Beast, those laws had been set down by Swash's grandfather long ago. "While you're on board my rig, everything you *think* you own belongs to me. That's the contract you signed."

"Your rules don't apply to me. I'm not your slave."

Even with a bum leg, Swash couldn't let the insolence stand. He straightened up and gently pushed Stitch out of the way. "Is that really the play you want to make? It's a long walk out of this desert."

"Are you honestly prepared to fight me?" Blade laughed.

Swash preferred not to lead through intimidation, but being the nice guy didn't work on everyone. He'd suspected from the moment he'd hired the thug that it might come down to a show of strength eventually. "Knives or fists?"

Blade set the shovel against the side of the Beast. He then pulled the knife from his belt and dropped it next to the shovel. "You don't know what you're starting here. I've fought my way out of a lot of armed camps."

The only reason opponents bothered listing their credentials was because they were scared, but that wasn't the only thing Swash's grandfather had taught him about fighting. Swash pulled out his knife and handed it Stitch. "Stakes?" he asked Blade.

"Okay." Blade stepped away from the vehicle and flexed

his arms as if he needed to limber them up. "If I win, I get to claim whatever I see fit out of a raid, get a say in our endeavors, and take possession of the jump spider as my prize."

Swash figured if Blade won, Swash might be the one walking out of the desert, so it didn't really matter if he accepted the man's demands. "And if I win, you do as you're told while on my crew, get paid an equal share to everyone else, get your cut when I say, and start calling me Captain."

Stitch backed up to the side of the Beast. Swash feared she might object to the contest, having just fixed both of them up, but she kept silent. Whisper had mentioned that Blade had dislocated his shoulder. If it was bothering him, he wasn't showing it. Swash wouldn't be able to hide his hip discomfort as easily, but that had its advantages.

Blade made an open-armed rush at Swash's waist. Without the maneuverability to avoid the bum-rush, Swash took the big man's momentum in the chest. The impact sent them tumbling into the sand. Blade was first back on his feet, but his second attack was met with a handful of sand in the eyes from Swash. As instinct made Blade cover his eyes, Swash lunged up on his good leg and landed a punch to the big man's stomach.

Even with his momentary lack of vision, Blade had Swash locked around the waist with his arm. The loose sand cushioned the blow of having the solid mass of masculinity land full force on top of Swash. Being pinned under Blade's legs didn't give Swash any wiggle room as the meat-hook-sized fist came crashing toward his face. With one arm, Swash deflected the blow, and with the other, he landed a stinging jab straight to the man's weakened shoulder.

The separation of bone from joint sent Blade tumbling into the sand. Swash lunged up then delivered a pile-driver elbow smash to Blade's chin. Blood gushed onto the white sand. "Had enough?" Swash leaned over Blade, panting from the battle.

Blade laughed, sending blood bubbles into Swash's face. "What kind of pansy-ass schoolyard fights have you been in?" He swung hard to the left, knocking Swash's arm out from under him and causing him to fall into the blood-soaked sand.

Swash knew he was in trouble the moment Blade sprang to his feet. As Blade swung his arms wide and lifted his foot, Swash had a perfect view of the sole of the big man's sand boot—a pattern that was sure to be emblazened on Swash's face. With both hands locked together into a single fist, he sent a blow at the toes of the work boot. Though his ploy didn't stop the strike, it did redirect Blade's heel down to Swash's chest. It also put the man's leg between Swash's arms. Grabbing the shoe with one hand and the man's calf with the other, Swash twisted on the sand like an alligator rolling his prey.

The dislocation of knee and hip had Blade screaming in anger. "You sand fracker!"

Swash wasn't about to let Blade up for another round. He got to his feet while still holding onto the man's boot. Blade screamed again. "Give up! I don't want Stitch wasting her time fixing anything more than she has to."

"I don't mind," Stitch said from the side of the Beast.

"I give up! Now, fracking let me go!"

Swash twisted the foot to remind Blade of the stakes.

"Captain!" Blade shouted, pounding the sand. The word seemed to have pained him even more than the dislocated leg.

Swash finally let go. "This had better be the end of it. If you double cross me, I'll get word to every trading post from here to the Canadian border of your treachery."

Blade rolled to his back. "I'll be loyal. You have my word, *Captain*."

Swash did his best to look nonchalant as he backed up to Stitch. "I think our friend here needs a little hammering back together." Though he didn't want to admit it in front of Blade, each word he spoke felt like a red-hot dagger in the center of his chest.

"I'll take him to the med bay," Stitch said. "Once I'm done with him, I'll check on you as well. That hip repair wasn't meant to withstand calisthenics."

Swash favored her with a half smile, hoping she'd deduced more about his condition than what she'd said.

17

Swash felt as beaten up as the Beast looked. Letting Blade take the jump spider for a survey of the area was equal parts foolishness and a test of trust. Putting only a gallon of go-juice in it, however, would mean even if the hired gun decided to jackrabbit on Swash, he wouldn't get far.

Stitch continued to stand at his side as if the fight hadn't proved anything regarding his physical condition. "That went better than I'd expected."

"I'm not sure if I'm supposed to take that as a compliment or an insult," he said.

"I just meant, you don't exactly come across as the violent type."

"Put it down to a lack of sleep." He activated his com link to Blade. "What are you seeing out there?"

"All clear—Captain."

In spite of the fight and promises, Swash hated having to

trust Blade. Sending up a drone to retrace the man's tire tracks, however, would mean an even longer delay out in the scorching desert. "Roach, fire up the engines."

"You've got it, boss." Without any change in tone, Roach managed to establish his authority over Blade with the single use of the more informal title.

The ground under Swash's feet rumbled as the big engines roared to life. In spite of the long run through the storm and having the rig buried in the sand, the engines sounded as fresh as if they were being fired up for the first time. Swash took Stitch's hand and led her farther from the dune. "Let's see how she does, Roach."

Sand puffed up from both sides of the Beast as the wheels made one full rotation. "I'm reducing speed and increasing the torque to full on both sides," Roach said.

The next rasping of rubber against sand had the monster-sized rig lurching forward. Sand fell behind the rear tires as if the desert were trying to hold the Beast in place. With another roar of the engines, she pulled away from the dune. Sand cascaded off the sides, piled onto the catwalk, and ran in rivulets through the open-walled tires. With one front wheel and the two rear ones angled, the Beast pivoted on the center wheels. She dragged her front tire, which was frozen in place by the splinted axle, reminding Swash of his own infirmity.

"That looks good, Roach. I think she's clear enough for us to work on. Blade, if you're comfortable that we're not being spied on, come on home. We'll need your strength to get this thing fixed up. While we're stationary, we can finish brewing the go-juice."

"On my way, Cap."

Swash smiled to himself. Everyone deserved a little consolation prize. Allowing Blade a less formal greeting, combined with a little alcohol inducement, would hopefully soothe any lingering hard feelings.

He leaned on Stitch's shoulder. "And now I think I'll take that nap you've been recommending."

BLADE STOPPED the jump spider on a dune overlooking the Beast but far enough away not to be noticed. He'd misjudged Swash Jones. That was the kind of mistake that might have gotten him killed in a marauder camp. Living with the rovers had made him soft. A weapon required battle to stay in top form, and the months of luxury had taken their toll on his reflexes.

"I should have pounded that guy's face. What was I thinking?"

Sure, Swash had proven to be a worthy leader, at least for rovers. *Captain.* Using the term was going to take some getting used to. He tapped the fuel gauge with his knuckle. The needle didn't move. One-quarter of a gallon of go-juice wasn't going to get him very far, and after circling the Beast, he hadn't come across any indications of marauders. Though that worked well for the crew, it limited Blade's options. He rested his head on his hands at the top of the steering wheel. Eight years of making his way by whatever means he could find had changed him.

It's not your fault that they're dead.

Eight years and a thousand miles away, he'd put up three gravestones on a hill overlooking a peaceful valley. The intervening space and time had made him grow hard, but every once in a while, like a dog at the end of a leash, he felt the emotional tether yank so hard against his throat that he found it hard to breathe.

Joining Swash's band of rovers had been one of those moments. The fools needed his help. That much was clear. But it wasn't the enticement of riches that swayed his decision. Even leaving the West Coast, which carried memories around every bend, hadn't mattered. What had made him sign on with Swash was his memory of the pride in Wave's eyes, now forever closed. The piece of his soul that she'd kept safe through their years of marriage ached like the phantom pain of a severed limb.

He kept his head on his hands, feeling like a stray dog that had been taken in and cared for. He couldn't leave. He wanted to. He really did. Life with the marauders had prevented him from thinking about Wave, Breeze, and Crash. The pillaging dulled the memory of their faces. Spending time with the rovers had resurrected their images to haunt his dreams. Memories of tilling the soil, raising food crops, and bartering with his neighbors were hardly terrors, but waking up to the new reality turned the sweet dreams of family sour.

He'd changed his name, his occupation, and the people he kept company with. Still, the moral noose around his neck remained. Fighting Swash had been less about railing against the man's rules than seeking a physical manifestation of his personal condemnation. It hadn't worked.

It's not your fault. He wondered if he'd have the same reaction when he lost the crew of the Beast.

He fired up the jump spider. He had work to do and people to protect. At least if he could inspire the crew's hatred, the emotional noose around his neck might not be as tight when they died. Those he cared about always ended up dead eventually.

---

18

*R*oach needed sleep, but he also needed to get the busted axle out of the transfer case. Swash wanted to get moving by nightfall, and Roach had no intention of letting the boss down. With the Beast lifted on its built-in jacks, accessing the rod of metal wasn't the problem. Figuring out how to release the electric motor that surrounded the shaft, unhooking the rod from the sealed gears, and getting it out of the wheel hub, however, taxed every bit of knowledge Roach had picked up about fixing drivetrains. Building the jump spider had been easy compared to figuring out all of the mechanisms inside the earth rover.

The initials and date scratched into the side of the axle—*SJ '47*—indicated that Swash had changed the same chunk of metal when he was still a kid. Roach wondered what disaster had fracked up the rod thirty-five years back and why they'd sent a kid who wasn't even ten under the Beast to fix it.

Roach unscrewed the final bolt on the constant-velocity joint. The hunk of metal came loose from the oversized hub. He inspected the mounting ring. Flipping the Beast onto one wheel should have done all kinds of damage, yet from what he could tell, only the axle had snapped. He added the question to his mental list of what he would ask Swash when they weren't fighting for their lives.

It felt good to outwork the boss for a change. Sleep aboard the rover had less to do with sticking to a schedule than completing whatever job desperately needed to be done so they could get back underway. For Swash, that meant sleeping was seldom an option. The fact that he'd turned over the responsibility to Roach was no small matter. He wiggled the second half of the busted shaft, trying to figure out why it wasn't coming loose. If the problem involved messed-up gears, they might have to limp along until the Beast could get a proper overhaul—not that Roach knew when or where that would be.

"If Swash could get you out when he was just a kid, this problem can't be solved with brute force." Roach pulled a long thin blade of metal from his repair kit and eased it along the shaft. The supplemental electric motor, a match to the one on the other five wheels, never seemed to need work. A click vibrated the strip of metal as the rod came loose. "There you are, you little dickens." With the second half of the shaft in hand, Roach worked his way out from under the rig.

Whisper stood alongside the wheel and handed him a

water bottle. "I thought you might be getting a little warm under there."

He looked into her eyes, trying to decide if the comment had been innocent or in regard to his body suit. "Thanks." The water had the brackish flavor of reclaim.

"I'm sorry about the taste. Stitch says she's saving the fresh water for barter."

He'd only tasted fresh water a couple of times in his life. Tahoe, though at one time one of the cleanest lakes in the world, had become a seemingly bottomless pond of algae. "It's fine."

She bit her lip, making her look even younger than she usually did. "Did you hear about the fight?"

"Yeah. Swash kicked Blade's hindquarters. He had it coming."

Whisper suddenly seemed to find something fascinating about her shoes. "Do you think he'll come back?"

Roach gazed out at the dunes, half expecting to see the cloud of sand indicating Blade's return. "I don't think he has much of a choice. The jump spider's range on a gallon of go-juice won't take him far."

"You don't trust him, do you?"

Blade reminded Roach of every bully who'd beaten up on the kid who was slightly odd, and in Roach's case there was no *slightly* about it. "Between the time I broke out of the basin and when I ran across Swash, I had more than my share of run-ins with people like Blade."

"That must have been a hard time for you."

He wondered how deeply she intended to fish into his psyche. "I got by as a thief. With my special skills, I could

149

climb walls, scamper along ceiling joists, and squeeze into areas most found impossible to access. Then, so long as I could get to the jump spider, I squirted out of town before anyone noticed me. I had to work with a lot of shady characters to move my bounty, but I found if I had enough to offer, those living on the edge weren't so concerned about abnormalities."

"Unlike the marauders?"

He'd done his best to avoid the armed camps. "Hate is like drug that affects everyone differently. For many people, it manifests as prejudice, and that bias works best against people they don't know."

"Gen mods."

He wondered how she'd managed to grow to adulthood without being subjected to the atrocities he'd witnessed. "Many don't even know we exist. You didn't. Those of us who did make it out do our best to hide who we are."

"But you didn't hide from Swash?" she asked.

"He's not the type of person you can keep secrets from for very long. He's a little like you in that regard."

Whisper blushed. "I didn't ask. You told me all on your own."

"Because I knew you'd find out eventually. Telling you meant I could get my story out before you started making assumptions."

"You're not worried about Blade making assumptions?"

He thought about making a snide comment regarding Blade's lack of awareness of others but thought better of it. "If he sticks around long enough, eventually, I'm sure it will come up. I'll be watching for the right opportunity to tell him."

"I'm glad you trusted me enough to tell me," she said.

She reminded him of himself during the years of sneaking around. His goal had always been to learn as much as he could without revealing anything he didn't have to. That time had taught him that asking questions often resulted in getting some in return. She had to expect him to ask.

"What about you?"

"What do you mean?" Whisper kept her eyes down.

"I know very little about you, in spite of vouching for you with Swash."

She finally looked up into his eyes. "Then why did you?"

He'd asked himself the same question many times. "I suppose I saw something of myself in you. I never was a slave, but when I ran into Stitch, I was on the run and in pretty bad shape. If she hadn't offered me help, I'm certain I wouldn't be here. She saved my life. I guess I was trying to pass on the favor."

Whisper nodded as if she were giving in to an internal argument. "My mother sold me."

Life was a commodity. Even Swash had made it clear that the people on board were ultimately his possessions, although Roach couldn't imagine him ever selling anyone. "Things must have been tough."

"That's not why she did it."

He could feel her desire to explain, but as with getting the axle out of the Beast, he had to slide the question in just so to get her to open up. "You can trust me."

"I know." She smiled. "But the secret isn't fully mine to tell. I'm searching for someone, and Mother thought I'd have a better chance of finding them if I was socially invisible. As a slave, I could pass in any society without too many questions asked."

"Have you found this person you're after?"

"No, but Mother wouldn't have contacted me unless she had information that I need to continue my quest. I know I'm putting everyone in danger, but what I'm doing is important. I wish I could tell you about it. Maybe when we get up the mountain, I will."

He had the sense that she was manipulating him. "And you wanted to make sure I was on your side. Is that it? Please tell me you're not blackmailing me. Because if you are, I've got enough pull with Swash to have you kicked off this rig."

She put her hand on his arm. "It's not like that. I would never tell your secret to anyone. Ever. You have to believe me." Tears glistened in her eyes.

Trusting others had gotten him into trouble in the past. He still wasn't sure it hadn't again when he'd listened to Stitch about revealing his secret to Whisper. "I vouched for you to get you on this rig. I don't know why, but I do know I would do it again if needed. As for continuing to back your request to climb those mountains, I'm not committing to anything."

"I'm not asking you to."

19

*T*he light above Swash's bunk flashed green, meaning all was good and it was time to get up. "Yep, I'm coming."

The gentle rocking of the Beast meant they were already underway. Stitch had no doubt convinced Roach to let him sleep in longer than he'd planned. Even with the bone mend that the medic had shot into his ribs and the drugs she'd insisted he needed to function, everything hurt. He looked down the bunk at his bare feet, wondering if it was worth the effort to put on shoes. Leaning forward and experiencing a sharp pain in both sternum and hip, he decided he could live without the boots.

He slid up the berth's protective cover. The lights in the living quarters were dimmed, indicating he hadn't been the only one asleep. He looked around the area that served as an activity catchall. The foldout kitchen at the back of the room, opposite Stitch's med center, had been stashed. The four rows of twin lounge chairs that served as workstations, protective seating during a rough ride, and entertainment modules were locked in their forward-facing position. Stitch and Blade's bunks had their Occupied lights glowing.

He eased down past Roach's empty berth. The kid needed rest. Stitch really shouldn't have let him push it that hard. She must have figured Swash's condition needed more time to heal than he'd expected.

He hobbled back to the dual washrooms, one beyond the kitchen and the other next to Stitch's medical center. He needed a shower but opted for a little cold water on his face and over his head. The idea of squirming out of his clothes sent pains all over his body. In the mirror, he looked like hell—sunken eyes rimmed in black, scars both recent and ancient, a three-day growth of beard that seemed to never change, and hints of gray at the temples of his untamed hair. He turned away from the mirror, grateful that he didn't have to stare at himself all day.

As he left the washroom, he instinctively put his hand on the door at the back that led to the machine shop. The area was Roach's domain now, but for most of Swash's life, it had been where he felt most at home. The engines that took up the center of the room were silent, meaning the Beast was running on electricity. He chose to leave well enough alone. Whatever pile of busted parts he found on the two benches that ran along the walls would just lead to another discussion with Roach about what needed to be patched together next.

He worked his way through the crew quarters while

trying not to bash into the berths and wake their occupants. When he got to the bridge, he saw it was pitch-black outside. "You should have roused me earlier."

Roach leaned back in the driver's seat, half turning toward Whisper, who was manning the drones. "I wanted to make sure the axle was fully operational before handing over the wheel. There was enough bar stock in the machine shop to work up a new one. Why didn't you tell me you were the one who replaced the last one?"

Swash closed his eyes, trying to envision being under the Beast, fighting with the frozen steel bar. "That was a long time ago. We were sliding down a mountain covered in snow and ice. My grandfather took an unseen boulder to the axle. I spent three days under there, trying to fix the fracking thing."

"Then I guess I should be grateful I only had to deal with heat and sand." Roach leaned over and pulled a crate from beside the driver's seat. "Blade dropped these bottles of whiskey off. He said you'd know what they were about. He actually referred to you as *Captain*."

Swash made a quick check of the contents—four bottles. "I guess our fight left an impression on him." He kicked the box toward the door. "On your way out, lock these in the storage pantry."

With the Beast cruising through the open sand, Roach groaned as he got out of the chair. He stretched his leg abnormally far to the side.

"You two have a nice chat?" Swash took the open seat. He didn't want to be too obvious in case he was wrong, but knowing who knew what helped him know which secrets to keep.

"He told me about being a gen mod." In her nightgown, Whisper lazed in the chair, looking like she'd gotten up in the middle of the night for a cup of hot cocoa and forgotten to return to her bunk.

"Is that something you can live with?" There had been plenty of people who'd learned of Roach's biology one way or another. Nearly every case had ended with Swash firing up the Beast for a hasty departure.

"We all have our secrets. Roach's is just a little juicier than most." Her expression lost some of its playfulness. "You can trust me. I'll never tell anyone."

Roach nearly folded his body in half as he reached down for the box. "I think I'll sleep for about a week. The last few days have been rather taxing, emotionally and physically."

Swash chuckled. "I can't give you a week, but so long as we're just a ship in the deep desert, hopefully, we'll catch a break."

Roach's voice faded as he headed toward his bunk. "Except for sandstorms or breakdowns or running out of fuel or stumbling across an enclave filled with danger…"

Swash checked the gauges. While Roach had been busy with repairs, the others had clearly finished brewing fuel. Both the plant oil and go-juice tanks read full. The only operational battery storage indicator wasn't as encouraging, showing it to be at only half charge. He tapped the gauge as if that would make a difference.

Whisper stretched up her arms. "Roach changed out solar panels one and two for three and four. It took longer than he'd hoped, which is why we're a little short on electricity."

Swash shook his head. "I'm sure he did his best." Three and four were usually only activated when the roof array was at full extension, making the Beast look like some monstrous bug about to take flight. They'd run fine with just the two so long as they didn't run into another storm. "What did he say about the damaged units?"

"Panel one is badly scratched. When the high-strength transparent safety shield blew away, there wasn't anything to stop the sand from blowing over the delicate plate. The thing is nearly opaque white."

That was irritating news. They could fabricate glass if they had to, but it wasn't easy. "But the cells underneath were okay?"

"The cells on two were okay, but panel one is toast."

Swash stared out the front view screen. Though solar had been the energy of choice in the west long enough to make the units easy to obtain, the crew wasn't exactly headed for prime trading posts. "Any hope your mother might have some panels up in that crow's nest of hers?"

"I don't know what's up there."

He suspected Whisper was lying. "I've put a lot on the line for this adventure of yours. You're going to have to do better than 'I don't know' if you expect me to continue. So far, all you've given me are numbers you heard on your headphones and an interpretation of the signal that I can't verify."

She looked at him with her big innocent eyes then turned back and closed the hatch to the rest of the Beast.

"It's been seventeen years since I've seen her. A lot can change in that amount of time." Whisper was equivocating, which probably meant she had valuable inside information but didn't want to lose her strategic advantage by sharing it.

"Let's start with what you remember," Swash said.

"My mother isn't just some tinfoil-cap-wearing egghead. She's Brigadier General Sky Payne. *And* she's a tinfoil-cap-wearing egghead. Believe it or not, there are still pockets of advanced civilization left in this world. She was educated in one of them."

Swash had heard of areas where the rich, powerful, and intelligent had found refuge during the last days of the war. If they'd managed to keep the cities a secret, so-called advancements like higher learning might have been passed from one generation to the next. The title indicated that Whisper's mother had spent her life in such a commune. Or Whisper's grandparents had *named* their daughter Brigadier General, which was just as plausible as her being a military leader.

"If that's true, how did you end up a slave?"

She looked at the door as if expecting someone to barge in. "I'm not supposed to talk about it."

By closing the door, she'd already tipped her hand. "Clearly, you're going to, so let's skip the song and dance and get down to the good stuff."

Whisper closed her eyes and nodded. "How much do you know about the old satellite network?"

He settled back into the chair, preparing for a long night. "Mostly what I heard from my grandfather. At one time, people relied on the global positioning satellites to tell them exactly where they were and where to go. During the wars, such reliance on technology for answers proved to be deadly. One side would hack the system and send false information to the other, causing a platoon to drive into an ambush or even straight off a cliff. Traveling by air was effectively ended without precise and reliable satellite positioning information. When people couldn't even count on where they were standing, losing faith in everything else transmitted by satellite wasn't a big leap. Satellites became as suspect and hated as nuclear power plants."

Whisper frowned as she nodded. "What you heard is half truth, half propaganda. The important part of your story is the shadowy hackers who overrode the systems. The software packages were meant to be impossible to tamper with. They had to be. Even when the system was being developed, the possibility of that level of hacking was the engineers' worst nightmare. But GPS was only one aspect of satellite communication. Imagine if things were different. What if, right now, you had access to weather imagery? You wouldn't need to worry about driving into a storm. Or if you were able to listen in to a city's communication network, you'd know where to hunt. Access to a satellite would give you unimaginable power, especially if you were the only one with the information. The sky would be the limit, literally."

He wondered how much of her story was the fairy tale she'd been told and how much she'd imagined. Since she had been sold into slavery as a young girl, he doubted anything she thought she knew was based on reality. "None of this is explaining why you were a slave. So far, it all sounds like the fanciful ramblings of a girl who doesn't want to believe that what happened to her was without reason. In my experience, most people became slaves when they were captured during the wars—bounty after a battle—or when they were offered as payment for a debt. And nearly every slave I've met had some sad story about how it had all been a mistake. You're entertaining, Whisper Payne, but not all that convincing."

If she couldn't come up with something more reasonable, once he got out of the deep desert, he'd head the Beast north along the foothills of the Rockies. There were always prime pickings where mountain runoff water intersected a temperate region suitable for growing crops.

"I'm not lying, Captain."

"I didn't say you were, but what you believe isn't necessarily so. You can be a bit fanciful at times."

She crossed her arms and glared at the view screen. "Just because I try to figure out what a singer was trying to say or what was going on just beyond what a picture captured doesn't mean I'm a starry-eyed romantic. I was raised by a military mother."

"One who sold you into slavery to find the key master. I remember. You have to admit, sending a little girl out into the world to find some mythical mad scientist sounds like something out of a children's story."

She kept her arms crossed as she looked over at him. "If that's true, then nearly my entire life has been a lie."

In his travels, he hadn't run across many people who believed in something larger than themselves. Even if Whisper's story turned out to be nothing more than hot air, he wasn't going to be the one to burst the balloon and let her hope dissipate into the bleakness of daily existence. "I suppose having a mission to hold onto beats facing the world with no motivation beyond basic survival. I hope we find the answers you believe in up on that mountain top."

20

Swash wasn't sure what to think of Whisper's story about her mother being a military commander. The truth was, he didn't really like to think about anything if he could avoid it. Coming up with preconceived ideas about what was ahead usually resulted in stuck thinking. He preferred to be more flexible in his outlook. As the sun crept over the desert toward the Beast, the mountains loomed large on the display screen. Rock tendrils stretched out from the foothills to the desert floor like an octopus feeling for prey.

With Whisper back in her bunk, he slid the top map out from the drawer. She hadn't trusted marking the location of the satellite dish on the page, but she had told him the coordinates. They were southwest of the dish. If he didn't make a change, they'd be at the base of her mountain by noon.

He pulled a measuring compass out and compared

where they were on the desert floor to the area Whisper had indicated. In a relatively short distance, the Beast was going to have to climb nearly two miles in elevation. She could do it, provided there was a path. Based on Whisper's explanation, he doubted there would be anything even remotely resembling an easy way up the cliffs and over the ravines to the summit. Military bases liked their security features, and one commanded by a techno-nerd wasn't going to be easy to sneak into. He tossed the measuring device on the table in frustration. Traversing the desert had been like crossing hell, but now that the end was in sight, he wondered if they had just stepped into an even more impossible situation.

The overhead weather gauges indicated a light wind from the south. Radiation levels were still in the tolerable range, but that wouldn't last if the winds grew in intensity. He needed to get off of the desert floor, where the straight line of storms could bury the Beast in fallout from the nuclear trench. So long as he kept to the north-facing ridges, he could at least alleviate that threat. The people who lived up there, the damage done during the wars, and the intensity of security systems that were designed to prevent people like Swash from climbing the mountain were the bigger threats.

He angled the Beast toward the north side of a rock outcropping. The bend in the mountain range would keep them out of the radiation's path for the time being and line them up with Whisper's mountain. A mile ahead, the hummingbird drone zipped across the sky in an attempt to maintain position ahead of the Beast.

Blindingly bright sunlit reflections sent to the visual overlay on the display screen made Swash lift his arm to his eyes. He slammed on the brakes before reaching for the display dimmer. From the rainbow of colors that lit up the cliff, adjoining rock pile, and debris field, the hummingbird looked to have suffered a serious malfunction. He hit the recall switch to bring the spaced-out bird home.

Stitch pushed her way past the partially closed hatch. "What the hell was that?" Her hair was tousled, and she held a hand to her forehead. Swash figured she hadn't woken up voluntarily.

"Sorry about the abrupt stop. Something's wrong with the hummingbird. It tried to blind me. My reflexes must have taken over."

The whirling ball covered in microcameras and fan blades sailed back into its chute as Stitch plopped down on the navigator's chair. "You're sure it's a malfunction?"

He reengaged the throttle. "I've only seen colors like that on a bad drug trip I once took down in the Baja Islands. I'll add the drone to Roach's pile of stuff needing repair. You can head back to your bunk if you want."

She pulled her robe up around her shoulders. "I'll keep watch, if you don't mind. Without the drone, you could use a second pair of eyes."

Swash leaned back in the chair. She was right. Without the drone, he felt like he was driving blind. As he rounded the corner, the impression became more than metaphorical.

"Sons of the rich!" He again slammed on the brakes and squeezed his eyes closed. This time, the bright light wasn't an overlay on the screen but was part of the outside world, as if some vehicle had turned its high beams on the rocky landscape.

Even with his eyes squeezed shut, he could tell the bridge had grown dark. Carefully, he tried prying open his lids. Stitch was lying halfway across the dashboard. "I found the dimmer."

"Thanks for that." Even with the room at lighting meant to imitate dusk, the iridescent rocks sparkled like prisms. "What do you think is causing this?"

She stood over him to read the exterior gauges. "I have no idea. It's not nuclear. Radiation is a little high but still within the safe zone. I've got solar goggles in medical. They should dull the light enough to head outside." She turned toward the hatch.

"While you're back there, you might as well roust the others."

As Stitch headed for the living quarters, Swash pulled his grandfather's journal tablet from the drawer under the maps. The old man had recorded everything. If he'd run across a field of glimmering rocks, he would have had something to say about it. Swash activated the screen and brought up the search window. *What would he have called it?*

He turned back to the Beast's front view screen. The rocks were still shimmering. He turned down the light even further until the cab was in full night mode. The cliff beyond the field of shiny rocks glowed a deep green. He punched *glowing green glass* into the search bar. A single listing came up: *Trinitite, nuclear obsidian.*

He tapped the heading. The face of his long-dead grandfather filled the screen. When the old man ran across something he couldn't explain, he often resorted to videoing instead of writing down his findings. "This stuff is more mythical than real. I've never seen it. According to the blind White Linen monk, when a nuclear bomb is detonated in a confined area, the silica in the rocks melt into glass, trapping other compounds. From what I could find, that much is based on fact. The myth part revolves around the monk's story of xenophobic societies in the mountains drilling blast holes and lowering nuclear explosives into them. When detonated, the bombs would cleave a mountain into a sheer, unscalable wall of glass. Since I've never seen one, that's all I've got." The screen went black.

21

With the eye protection and heat suit on, Swash felt like he was stepping out onto another planet. At least Stitch hadn't demanded that they wear breathing apparatus. The sun had moved far enough over the desert to light the cliff into a wall of flaming green. Though the glass layer was translucent, Swash couldn't tell how deep it extended into the mountain of granite.

"It's pretty." Whisper turned one of the green rocks like she was looking for some magic genie inside.

"Did you know about this stuff?" Swash didn't like surprises, especially when he'd put his crew's lives on the line.

She shook her head. "I didn't grow up on this mountain. Like I said last night, my mother kept it a secret."

One thing at least was clear to Swash—the girl hadn't been making the whole thing up. Whoever was up on the ridge above the glass cliff didn't want visitors.

Blade threw a rock toward the cliff. "How would someone even create something like this? I mean, I get your grandfather's explanation, but this would take precision blasting and a frack ton of nuclear ordinance."

Though he hadn't known about trinitite, when it came to nuclear material, Swash knew more than he wanted to. With a grandfather who'd been in the wars and a map of the country with an inexplicable no-go zone, any kid was bound to ask questions. And having been the boy hearing the stories, Swash had more than his fair share of images to haunt his dreams. "This area of the old states was never considered valuable. The one thing the southwest desert did have in abundance was uninhabitable land for storing nuclear waste. For a time, it seemed like every state in the union was sending trainloads of the stuff to the desert. When the states weren't bound to each other anymore, the leaders of this area no longer felt the need to sit on the stuff while their populations slowly died of cancer. The original laboratories that played around with nuclear weaponry are southeast of us."

"As is the nuclear trench," Stitch said.

Swash picked up one of the glass chunks. "The good news is that as glass, it's not very radioactive." He gazed past the field of sharp rocks to the shining greenish-black wall. "The bad news is we'll never be able to drive up a sheer cliff of glass."

Roach hammered one of the fist-sized jewels against another. They chipped into razor-sharp shards. "These rocks would slice the Beast's tires to ribbons before we were half a mile from that cliff."

Swash tossed the chunk of glass and turned to the crew. "Give me options. Nothing is too outlandish. Stitch, as medic, you start."

She turned away from the cliff. "We can't go back, and we can't go forward. That leaves north or south. The growing storm from the south is proof enough of the radioactive danger. So south is out, and even staying put is dangerous. By my calculations, we've got maybe two days before the storm sends debris from the nuclear trench so intense that we won't be able to step outside the Beast. Anyone have any thoughts on heading north?"

Whisper arched her back and neck as if trying to see her mother standing on top of the mountain. "Is there a way up the mountain if we go north?"

"North is out," Blade said. "The warlords have been at each other's throats for so long they torture any unknown intruder to death without even bothering with an interrogation. One of the armies up there isn't even human. I never want to face those monsters again. I'd set our chances at one in seventy-five that we'd be able to meet someone high enough to negotiate passage through the area before being killed. My vote is to go back the way we came. That city where we picked up provisions would make a sweet little trading post. We could live like kings and queens there."

"Then you're going without me," Stitch said. "I was lucky to keep you alive last time. I run an analysis on every city we pass through, just in case we do end up backtracking. There's a good reason the marauders have stayed clear of that area. That virus's mutation rate is thirty-six hours.

Anyone who stayed there would need to be pricked every day. Eventually, I'd either get the inoculant wrong, or the microbastards would outfox me. Either way, I can't see us surviving more than a week in that environment."

"Even if we could survive," Swash said, "I strongly suspect Scorch has already been notified of our visit to the town." He turned away from the others and walked to Roach, who remained in the field of glass, staring at the reflective cliff. "What's your take?"

Roach lifted a finger toward the mountain like he was trying to hold his place on a written page. "We could do it, boss."

"What are you talking about?"

He finally turned away. His voice had the far-off tone of someone who'd been hypnotized. "I haven't figured out how to roll the Beast's tires over this field of glass shards, but the real hard part is scaling the cliff. That we can do. I can climb that face. I know I can. It's glass, but it's not smooth. With the proper gear, I could latch onto the tops of the crystal-like columns and work my way to the summit."

Swash wondered if the kid had finally lost his mind. "Then what? Even if you did rope us all in with you, what about the Beast? I'm not just leaving her down here for someone to steal or to get pummeled by radioactive winds."

"We take her with us." His voice grew in pitch and tempo as he got into his idea. The others had already gathered around. "First, we change the cannon tip on one of the plasma lances for a cutting head. With a grappling hook and rope, I can work my way up, say, fifty feet. Then I drill a hole in the cliff. We can't cut glass, but we can melt it. I've got some titanium bar stock that would work like crampons in the holes. Next, we hook up the first winches from the front of the Beast to the rod. I climb another fifty feet and set the second crampon. The way I figure it, we use all three of the Beast's front winches for safety. Each of those hoists is rated at fifteen tons. Together, all three would more than handle the Beast's weight. With three lines, we'd have plenty of redundant support if something were to snap. And with different lengths on the cables, we'd have more than enough lift. Then she can drive straight up the cliff. When she reaches the lowest crampon, you pull it out and send it back up to me. That way, we can work straight up the mountain."

Swash held up another glass rock as if Roach hadn't already seen it. "This is glass. The plasma lance won't work on glass. It needs metal to arc the electricity."

Roach took the chunk from his hand and held it up to the light. "Before it melted, it was granite. Most of granite is quartz, which accounts for the glass, but this chunk is also radioactive, which means metal inclusions. Look at it, Swash. There are sparkly flecks in there. When the quartz melted, so did the iron. The lance can work with that. It's at least worth a shot."

The logistics were almost more than Swash could keep in his head at once. "Have you considered how much electricity that would require? Aren't you the one who's constantly giving me grief for pulling the trigger on the plasma cannon?"

"So we extend the full solar array. I know there are some damaged panels, but I'm not talking about constant discharge through the lance. There will plenty of time climbing and preparing the next crampon, which will give the batteries a chance to recharge. Plus, we'll be scaling a mountain, not racing through the desert using the electric motors. Worst case, you have to engage one of the multifuel engines as a generator."

"You are one crazy gas fracker," Blade said. "We're just going to drive right up the face of the cliff. That's what you're proposing? Assuming you can climb a wall of razor-sharp glass—which I doubt—how are you going to haul the plasma lance while you're free-climbing?"

"With your help." Roach bounced on his toes like he was already working the mountain. "I'll need you driving the jump spider as a moving work platform. She's lightweight and has her own winch. Once I climb the rope to the grappling hook and get into position, I'll use a line to pull up the lance. You'll be responsible for handling the power cord down to the Beast and replacing any busted drilling parts."

Swash's heart was already in his throat at the thought of driving the Beast straight up a cliff. "I said no idea was too outlandish, but so far, Roach holds the record for insanity."

Whisper continued to stare at the top of the mountain. "It would be the most direct route."

Blade shook his head as if to say they were all crazy. "Assuming for just a second that this was possible, the blast wall wasn't built for nothing. Whoever is up there is protecting something, and they don't want anyone creeping up on them. Hanging off the side of a cliff on a rope seems like a perfect spot to have rocks dumped on us. Have you thought of that? They could just stand up there and drop stuff on us all day."

Whisper stood with her fists at her sides. "My mother wouldn't let that happen."

Blade snapped his head toward her like he was itching for a fight. "That's assuming she's on the side of the people standing guard. We have no idea what's going on up there."

Whisper clenched her jaw and slowly nodded. "So someone needs to go up there and find out. I'll do it. Roach can take me up there then come back down to get the Beast." Swash wondered if whatever insanity had affected Roach was contagious.

"You don't want much, do you?" Blade asked. "He just climbs up the mountain with you, unseen, then drops you off, repels back down, then does it all over again with the Beast. You're crazy."

Roach shook his head. "Whisper's right, but I can do it alone. There's no point in risking both of our lives."

Whisper kept her fists to her hips. "And how do you expect to find my mother? Even if you did manage to spot her troops, they'd consider you an intruder. You'd have a bullet in you before you had a chance to explain. I'm the only one she trusts from below."

"Well, I'm not leaving you up there alone," Roach said. "I'll take you up then lower a line. Blade can use the rope for the jump spider. The plan will still work without us. Blade runs the jump spider up our support line from the top of the cliff and drills the holes. Swash drives the Beast, and Stitch works the winches and retrieves the crampons. It'll be tight, but it will work."

Swash could feel that it was decision time. "I don't run a democracy, but I'm also unwilling to demand that you all risk your lives without at least having your say. As for me, I'm inclined to go with Roach's plan. Every other direction seems to end in death."

"I trust Roach," Whisper said. "I know he can do it."

"I think the whole idea is gas-fracking crazy," Blade said. "There's no way that anyone could climb that cliff of glass. Not that it matters. I haven't heard any plan that gets us across this field of razor glass."

Swash scratched the back of his neck. The itching usually preceded him doing something he knew he'd regret. "About that. The scale-plate armor that protected the underside of the Beast is removable. It turns into long treads that can be wrapped around the tires. With the protection in place, the Beast can roll across practically anything. The overlapping sheets of metal also give her better traction. It results in an uncomfortable ride, but it should work."

Stitch walked up to Roach, took his hand, and led him farther into the field of rocks. Whatever she said made him audibly catch his breath. He pursed his lips and slowly nodded.

She turned toward the rest. "I'm on board."

Roach locked eyes with Blade. "You've got a right to know why I can scale that cliff. I'm a gen mod. Those monsters you ran into up north were probably gen mods also. If this is going to be a problem between us, I'd rather have it out now than while either of us is dangling off a cliff."

Blade gutted out a laugh. "You're a fracking drill hole. There's no way you're a mutant. Those monsters I ran into didn't even look human. I don't know what you're trying to pull, but it ain't funny."

Roach looked from Swash to Stitch then to Whisper. "I'd rather not have to pull off my clothes again."

"It's true, Blade." Whisper tiptoed through the field of rocks to stand next to Roach. "He showed me. I'm okay with it. Actually, I think it's kind of sexy." She looked down, bit her lip, and gazed up out of the corner of her eye at Roach.

"Now you're just trying to make me sick," Blade said.

She continued looking at Roach but answered loud enough to be heard by everyone. "I'm serious." She held out a finger. "Most guys only use one appendage, and they're not very creative with it. Just in and out like a toilet plunger. I've always been more attracted by what a guy could do with his hands—caressing, massaging, teasing. And instead of the two that humans are limited to, Roach has four. Now, that's sexy."

"Stop," Blade said. "I don't know what sick game you all are playing, but I'll agree to tackle the mountain if you all will just give it a rest. I'm not falling for your foolish prank."

22

*R*oach pulled the old Kevlar suit from his storage locker. Back in his thieving days, the black-and-gray outfit had been equal parts protection, camouflage, and superhero costume. It stretched and moved in ways a normal human body suit couldn't. *Thanks, Mom. I promise to make you proud.* The memory of getting the present just before boarding the jump spider for the ride out of the basin was one that crept up on him every time he pulled out the protective clothing.

He rolled it up tightly and forced it into his tote bag. A superhero had to play the role of either a normal human or an oddity but never both at the same time. When he closed the locker, he discovered Swash standing on the other side of the metal door. The roll of cable over his shoulder looked new.

"It's the lightest stuff I could find that would do the job."

Roach hoisted the coil that would need to be hauled all

the way to the top of the cliff then tossed down to be used by the others. "This ain't gonna be easy."

"It's not too late to change your mind. You know I'll cover for you," Swash said.

The downside of being a superhero was that the jobs were never easy. In fact, they needed to appear impossible for the average human. "Then what? Face it, boss, we don't have any good options. Just give me the grappling hook." Once Roach got an idea, there was no turning back.

"Blade is pulling it out of the jump spider."

Stitch led Whisper out of the med bay. With her hair tied back and in all-black climbing gear, Whisper looked like a completely different person. "Will this work?" the girl asked.

Roach handed her the tote bag. "Only one way to find out. As soon as Blade shows up with the hook, we need to get moving. I want to be at the base of the mountain before it gets dark. I hope you're ready for a long night."

Stitch dropped a backpack at Roach's feet. "Water, food, and medical supplies. I doubled up on the gauze and coagulants. There's also a testing kit for air pathogens and insects. Your best bet is to snag a mosquito if possible."

Roach stared at the sack and shook his head. "Stitch— no. I'm already hauling Whisper and a mile of cable up that mountain. When I first proposed the idea, it was to go alone. I can't carry that sack and scale the glass cliff at the same time. I'm sorry, but this is where I draw the line."

She looked down at the bag, pursing her lips. Finally, she reached in and pulled out two water bottles and a couple of rolls of medical tape. "I've loaded this liquid up with as much stimulant and as many nutrients as I could keep in suspension. It doesn't look like much, but there should be enough in these bottles to keep you both going for twenty-four hours. Hopefully, you'll be able to find something once you get off the cliff. If you're unsure about what you find up there, stick it in the empty water bottle and toss it down to me. I'll signal you with what I find. One flash for safe, two for okay in moderation, and three for dangerous."

Roach nodded as he stuck the bottle in his belt loop and the roll of tape in his pocket. If either of them got cut while on the cliff face, they wouldn't have time to rummage around in the backpack. "Thanks for understanding."

Blade came in through the back door. He dropped a dusty leather satchel on the closest lounge chair before taking the loop of rope and the hook off his shoulder. "How are you set for weapons?"

Whisper pulled the knife from her belt. "Just this, but I don't expect trouble up there."

Roach wasn't interest in discussing his equipment like some kid on his first campout. "I'm fine."

Blade opened the old bag and took out a long thick knife. "Take this with you."

Roach already felt like he was carrying too much equipment. "Either things will be hunky-dory up there, like Whisper believes, or we'll be dealing with a sizable military force. In either case, that knife isn't going to do me any good. But I do appreciate the offer."

Blade thrust the sheathed weapon into Roach's hand. "Just take the damn thing. I'm in charge of security. Be glad

I'm not forcing a blaster on you." He turned, lifted his bag, and headed out the back.

"I guess that's his way of expressing concern," Stitch said. "He does have a point, though. All of our lives are in your hands."

Swash let out a deep breath. "Get up there, secure our climbing zone, then toss the cable. Between the heat of day and the dangers from above, we'll only be able to lift the Beast up that cliff at night. You've got twenty-four hours. The storm's coming, and I can't risk hanging out here for an additional night. If I don't see the cable dangling from the cliff by nightfall tomorrow, I'm going to have to fire up the engines and make a run for it. There's no telling how long it would be before I could come back and rescue you two. You'd be on your own."

Roach doubted there was another captain who would even think of returning for a pair of lost crew members. Danger had a way of cracking the whip, driving a rover forever forward. "I won't let you down."

"You never have."

Roach made a final check of Whisper's climbing gear. "Time we got moving."

The last rays of the sun were still reflecting off the top of the glass cliff as they left the rover. At the edge of the pile of glass rocks, Roach again wished he were taking the trip alone. On all fours, he could scamper across the scree while keeping his weight evenly distributed on four points, unlike the human requirement of walking on two feet.

"I'm not going to ask if you really want to do this," he said. "You'd just insist you have to. And I'm not going to say

I'll leave you behind if you get hurt, because that would be a lie. We're in this adventure together."

She slipped her hand into his. "I'm braver than you think."

He gave her hand a quick squeeze before letting go. "Time to get our game faces on." He tested each step on the knife-edged rocks before trusting his weight to the movement. It would be a long haul across the scree. Time was against them, but he didn't dare hurry his steps and risk guiding Whisper to her doom. A rockslide, tumbling fall, or simple misstep could result in deadly cuts. With his fake-body suit and its heavy padding, he had less to worry about than she did.

"Your support in making this mission happen means a lot to me," she said, following in his footsteps.

He wondered if she realized the danger they were in. "Thank me when we get to the top of the ridge. And don't let that hook bang against the rocks."

Whisper set one prong over her shoulder. "How long do you think it will take to get to the top?"

Roach stopped and turned toward her. "Much as I enjoy talking with you, right now, I need my wits about me. Keep low, pay attention, and don't get hurt."

She nodded. "Sorry."

At the base of the cliff, Roach took the tote from Whisper's shoulder. "I need to change out of this body suit. Then I'll double-check your harness. You might want to down some of Stitch's concoction before we start the climb."

She bit her lip as her eyes remained on him. "Do you mind me watching?"

Even the whores he'd been with in the trading camps had left him alone until he was ready for them. He'd never blamed them. The sight of someone shedding his flesh wasn't exactly sexy.

He unlatched the work overalls. "Why would you want to?"

"I'm fascinated." She quickly looked back at his eyes as if she'd said something wrong. "I mean, not in a pervy way. I just have a hard time imaging what life must have been like for you—constantly hiding who you are, always afraid to let anyone get close, slinking in the shadows, surviving on whatever you could take."

He opened the chest zipper. "You make me sound like a scared mouse. If I'd been that timid, I never would have left the basin."

"Why did you?"

He struggled to get his narrow shoulders free of the suit. "Some days, I have trouble answering that question. Life with my people wasn't all that bad. Rain kept our water reserves filled. By drying algae from the lake and using it for fertilizer, we turned the soil into something that could grow crops. No one questioned who I was. Life was reasonable. But I guess no matter how comfortable or big a prison is, no one wants to live in a cage."

Her eyes fell to his arms and torso as he wiggled out of the foam suit. "Did you ever think of going back?"

Roach tried to ignore her gaze as he slipped the suit past his waist and down his legs. "Before I teamed up with Swash, sure. Those years on my own were tough. I didn't know who to trust, how to move what I stole, or where I could buy provisions so I didn't have to steal them." Roach folded up the suit and forced the air out of it. Fully collapsed, the thing needed to fit in the same tote he'd pulled the Kevlar from. "Swash was the one who found someone who could make a body suit. That first one was pretty crude, but once we put some clothing over it, I could pass in normal society."

"But there was no one back in the basin who drew you home?"

He slipped into the protective outfit. After he'd endured months at a time in the bulky body suit, the formfitting Kevlar allowed him to breathe a little easier. "I'd rather not talk about my time in the basin. Now, turn around so I can check that harness. I'm not risking you falling out of the thing halfway up the mountain."

23

Roach felt along the rounded corner of the twenty-foot-tall glass post. Wind-driven sand had etched the southern edges, but the north-facing section was as crystal clear and sharp as if it had been newly fractured. Even when he was wearing Kevlar gloves, free-climbing was too risky. He lifted the grappling hook and line from the ground and heaved it to the top of the pillar. The sharpened point failed to find something to grab onto, sending the line and metal crashing back down.

"There have to be notches and breaks up there. I just have to snag one."

"You can do it," Whisper said from behind the boulder.

Though he'd been talking more to himself than to her, the words of encouragement forced him to smile. He lobbed the hook upward again. This time, it bit firmly into the cliff.

He waved her over. "Tie the end of the line to the ring at your waist. You'll need to hold the excess rope taut while I climb. After I reach the first ledge, I'll throw the hook again and climb to the second. Once I'm up there, I'll haul you up to the first one. All you have to do is hold the line and use your feet against the cliff. So long as you don't graze your ankle or leg against the glass, you should be fine."

She nodded while looking into his eyes. "Be careful."

With a jump, he grasped the line as high as he could reach and started climbing hand over hand and foot over foot. When he reached the base of the metal hook, he lifted his leg over his shoulder, landing his foot on the ledge. With one good pull, he was balanced on the one-foot square patch of flat glass. There wasn't much room to maneuver, but he could manage. But he worried about what Whisper would use as support.

He pulled out the knife Blade had forced on him and slid the tip along the ridges and grooves in the glass. "This was a really bad idea." He kept his voice quiet enough that she wouldn't hear him.

"You can do it." Her words drifted up from below.

His knife stuck in a crack. It wouldn't provide much support, but in his desperation, he saw it as a lifeline to grab onto. Holding the handle, he leaned back as far as he dared and swung the hook to the next ledge. When it took hold, he looked down at Whisper and gripped the knife, showing her how she was going to have to support herself on the ledge.

She nodded her understanding as she grasped the handle of the knife tucked into her belt. With the heavy coil of line over one shoulder and the tote over the other, she would need every bit of support she could leverage. He looked up at his next destination, hoping to focus on the task at hand and not the dangers. When the line went taut, he scurried up the rope.

The ledge was even less secure than the one below. He could get his toes to grip, but an overhang made it impossible to swing up to the surface. With one hand holding the line and his toes grasping the lip, he reached out with his free hand. He felt along the scalloped north-facing edge. By keeping his hand bent and only his fingertips pressed into the shallow indentations, he avoided the irregularly shaped sharp edge. There was no way Whisper would be able to find support at that level. The two grip points allowed him to place his dangling foot against the sheer wall and take his weight off the rope.

Gingerly, he lifted the hook from its purchase. He could only barely make out the next ledge he'd mentally mapped out from the desert floor. *What was I thinking?* He forced the self-doubt from his mind and tossed the hook. It came sailing down without touching the cliff.

He held on tightly with fingertips and toes as the heavy chunk of metal dropped past him. As the line ran through his hand, he gradually applied pressure to slow its descent. He feared a sudden stop might jerk him off his perch.

From far below, he heard Whisper catch her breath. "Are you okay?" Her words were barely louder than the swinging line.

"I'm fine. Don't let anything fall on you." He yanked the line to his teeth then switched his handhold on it to bring the hook closer. When he had only a few feet of rope between his hand and the hook, he threw it with more determination. The sharp point bit into the cliff with a resounding crack.

Before Whisper could take up the slack, Roach pulled hard on the rope to free himself from the awkward hold. The higher he went, the more determined he grew. The ledge he hopped onto was so wide and deep, compared to where he'd just been, that it felt like a living room.

He leaned over the side. "Okay. Time to bring you up. This is a good one, so I'll haul you all the way to me. If you need a break at the lower ledge, let me know. Remember, just use your feet on the cliff face and hang on tightly to the rope. Don't get cut."

She nodded, put the loop of metal line over her head and shoulder, and gripped the rope. "I'm ready." Her trusting tone sent a lump into his throat.

Though not deep enough to be considered a cave, the indentation gave him something to lean into while keeping his hands over the lip of the ledge. If the rope rubbed against the sharp edge, Whisper wouldn't make it ten feet off the ground before it shredded. With one hand, he held the line close to his body and with the other pushed the slack out over the lip. Hand under hand, he worked the rope as if winding it onto a spinning wheel.

The trick was to not count how many times he lifted the cord or estimate how much was coiling at his feet. He was a machine lifting a weight, nothing more. Thinking about the girl at the end of the line would create emotions, and emotions had a way of disrupting fluidity of motion.

"I'm almost at the lip." Whisper's voice sounded like it was at his toes.

When he saw the top of her head, he slowed his retrieval of the line. She was closer to the cliff than he'd have liked, but her hands were still fixed to the rope. "Don't let go. I know it's tempting to grasp the ledge, but don't do it. You need to walk your way over."

She put the soles of her shoes to the edge and bent her knees while holding fast to the rope. As the rope went slack in his hands, she threw her arms around his neck. "Maybe this wasn't such a good idea."

He pulled out of her embrace. "Oh, it was a horrible idea." He tossed the hook as high as he could. The next ledge was a good thirty feet above their heads, and they didn't have time to savor the small victory.

As the sky went from black to dark blue, Roach's arms and legs felt like stretched-out rubber bands. "One more ascent."

On the ledge below him, Whisper had her back pressed to the cliff face, her hands on the wall, and her eyes closed. "I never want to do anything even remotely like this ever again in my life."

"Noted." He heaved the rope in a long arc toward the top of the cliff. A soft landing emanated down the line, far different from the harsh vibration of every other landing during the night. His heart started pounding in excitement. "I've hit something soft, probably a tree trunk. We're almost done, Whisper. Just hang on for a little longer." He leapt off the glass ledge and pulled as fast as his arms and legs would carry him. With each tug, the rope felt more secure. It wasn't until he swung over the lip that he saw the frayed section that had worn against the sharp cliff top.

Stupid. I should have felt the line rubbing against the glass knife-edge. He lay flat on the dirt and held the rope below the damage. Any additional tug from Whisper would break the line, but telling her would only cause her to panic. Roach's position over the cliff made it hard to haul on the line. She was going to have to help. He peeked over the edge. "I'm going to need you to climb the rope."

Her hair flew side to side in what must have been an emphatic *no*. "I can't." Her words trembled up to him.

He looked around for some alternative. Though the hook had latched onto the ironlike trunk of a desert shrub, the bush wasn't close enough to grab while holding onto the line down to Whisper. If he let go and she tugged too hard, he might lose his only connection to her. He did, however, manage to reach the end of the grappling hook and tease it loose. He could only hope there was enough line to get it down to Whisper. If he could just lighten the load, he'd have a much better chance of hauling her up.

"I'm lowering the hook to you. All you have to do is put the coil of cable onto it. I'll haul it up first. You can do it, Whisper. Just hold onto the rope up to me with one hand and lower the cable onto the hook with the other. Okay?"

Her ponytail bounced up and down, but he couldn't be certain of her response until he heard the soft, "Okay."

While still holding the section of rope below the fray with one hand, he gingerly lowered the hook with the other. The metal spike rolled gradually toward Whisper, teasing the coil of cable against her side. The rope down to her tensed as she pulled on it, as if letting go with one hand required twice the effort with the other. She seemed to be moving in slow motion. The coil fell from her shoulder.

Roach dug his toes into the dirt as he saw the heavy spool of line swing the grappling hook out from the cliff. If the coil came back and hit Whisper, she wouldn't be able to maintain her position. *Sons of the rich!* With every bit of strength he had left, he heaved on the line to the hook while trying not to transmit his fear down the rope ending in her hands. The weight dragged him closer to the cliff. He spread his legs to increase his resistance against the soil. The ankle of one foot bashed against the dirt-covered inner edge of the cliff. The glass razor bit through the Kevlar of the leg and into the knuckles of his handlike feet.

He didn't have time to worry about the injury. Grabbing the rope with his teeth, he quickly repositioned his hand and yanked on it a second time. He had to get the metal coil higher than Whisper's head. As the heavy circle crashed against the glass cliff, he closed his eyes and pulled so hard he ended up on his back with a foot and leg against the ledge. One arm was over the lip, holding the line to Whisper, and the other over his chest, grasping the rope to the coil while he prayed not to feel the thud of metal to flesh.

The coil swung in a long arc. From her firm hold on the rope, it was clear she was still in position but hadn't needed to trust her full weight to the line. *One disaster averted, but I still need that damn coil.* He desperately wanted to let go of the rope to Whisper—pulling it hand over hand, he could have the cable up the cliff wall with little effort. As it was, he feared even moving.

He took a moment to catch his breath. "You okay down there?"

"Just get me off this ledge. Please, Roach. I'm scared."

I'm scared too, he thought, but he couldn't afford to let her know that. "I've got you. I'm not letting go. It'll take me a moment to get everything ready."

"Okay." Her trembling trust encouraged his heart if not his mind and limbs.

He eased the toes of his undamaged foot out of the dirt. With the rope to the cable across one thigh, he bent his other leg until he could hook it with his heel. His injured foot provided his only real support. He felt like the toes were being cut off as his body slid closer to the edge. The sharp lip was cutting him all the way from the ankle to the side of his ribs. *Frack you, I'm not giving up.* He curled his foot-hand around the rope and pulled it hard to the hand at his chest. The success of gaining a couple of feet of line strengthened his willpower. With the new handhold on the line, he eased his foot back to the cliff edge and yanked up another section. Foot to hand, he drew the coil up. When his toes encountered the hard metal shaft of the grappling hook attached to the roll of cable, he took another breather.

He'd been so focused on lifting it that he hadn't considered how to get it over the lip. Almost as if it were working on its own, his foot returned to a position against the inside of the cliff wall. "This is gonna hurt." He shoved his heel against the glass, forcing his body away from the lip and pulling the coil over the top without letting go of the rope down to Whisper. The action also pulled her off her ledge. "Hang on, Whisper. I'll have you up here in a jiffy."

He dropped the hook and coil on the ground next to his body then quickly turned his full attention to the frayed rope with the girl at its end. His hands worked like a power winch. With each foot of lift, he imagined Whisper dangling at the end of the line, her life literally in his hands.

The moment her head crested the ridge, she dove forward, rolling on top of him. "My hero." There wasn't even a hint of sarcasm in her voice.

24

Whisper fell on her back, grateful to be off the cliff of razor glass. "I thought for sure we were going to die."

Roach took her by the shoulders, rolled her toward him, and gazed into her eyes. "Always think *for sure we're going to live*. That's how you survive."

Her relief at being off the wall of terror only lasted until she saw the smear of blood that covered Roach's leg and side. "You're hurt."

He pointed at the tote over her shoulder. "You need to get me into my body suit. Once it's around me, it contracts. It'll stop the bleeding."

His voice was far too soft and breathless for her to believe the damage wasn't serious. She pulled out of his hands then yanked open the sack. The cumbersome body suit inflated as it unrolled. Out of curiosity, she slipped her hand inside. Each touch her fingers made to the inner lining was reflected in a movement by the exterior fake muscles. *That must be why it looks so real when he's wearing it.* She tried not to let the mental rambling slow her from helping Roach. Holding out the chest, she drew it around his feet.

He scrunched his eyes closed and contracted every muscle under her touch. "You have to get the Kevlar off first. With the long cut, it should peel off me like a banana skin. You'll have to get everything off for the body suit to fully enclose me. We don't have time for modesty."

"Right." The warrior persona that her mother had tried so hard to instill in Whisper took over. Roach was in trouble, and she was his only hope. Gently, she split the Kevlar along his side, revealing Roach's fine sweat-soaked monkey hair. From the amount of blood he was losing, she knew she had to move fast. "Tell me what to do, Roach."

He reached down and tore the shreds of fabric from his skin. "Use the med cloth Stitch gave us. Run it along my wounds, then get me into the body suit." His voice lost volume with each word.

She pulled the roll of white tape from her pocket and pressed the end to his ankle. With one hand on the inside of his leg, she used the other to smooth the line of cloth against his outer leg. She ran the medical bandage up his calf, thigh, hip, and finally rib cage. Though he was thin and wiry, his muscles felt like bands of steel under her touch.

"It seems to be holding." She cut off the remainder of the roll.

He held out his hand, revealing rope burns on his palm. "Better wrap my hand and foot while you've got the tape handy, then we need to get me into that suit."

The red stain on the ground indicated that he'd lost more fluid than the small water bottle could replace. She quickly stemmed the bleeding from the remaining gashes. He slid into the suit like he was easing into a sleeping bag. The impression made her work faster, as she had a budding fear that he was preparing for a permanent slumber.

She pulled the bottle of enhanced fluid from her belt. There was only a finger's worth sloshing at the bottom. "Drink this. I need to find you some water."

He took the bottle but shook his head. "No time. Find your mother first." After draining the bottle, he tossed both of the empties to her. "You'll want these in case you find anything drinkable during your journey."

Whisper stashed the bottles in her belt then looked up at the sun-dappled ridge. Scaling the glass cliff had only gotten them halfway to the summit. Both the military and scholastic sides of Sky Payne would demand that her headquarters be located as high as possible. Armies always prized the high ground, and listening and locating satellites required as much unimpeded sky as possible. "I have to climb to the top."

Roach pointed at a tumble of boulders. "I can hide in the shade under there. Help me with this gear, then sweep the area clean of our presence. Once you're sure I'm well hidden, get moving. We don't have a lot of time."

SHE HATED LEAVING ROACH. He was in a bad way and needed her help, but the best way to get him the medical care he required was to move the plan forward. *He'll be okay. He has to be.* She turned her attention to the climb ahead. It wouldn't be easy, but then nothing ever was when it came to dealing with her mother.

The last time Whisper had seen the woman, Sky Payne had been a young captain in the Renegade Army. Somewhere among the dozens of peaks that stretched out along the mountain range was the one Whisper had called home—the one her mother had been in charge of defending. The scrub brush, granular-quartz-covered ground, and rough boulders she was facing weren't that different from what Whisper remembered as a girl.

Nine years old had been far too young to be sent out on her own, no matter the situation. Over the intervening years, she'd only talked to her mother sporadically, just enough for each of them to keep tabs on what the other was doing. Secrecy was part of Whisper's mission, though as a child, learning that she was about to serve a cause greater than herself hadn't eased the blow of being sold into slavery.

To survive, she'd split her soul into three pieces. There was the innocent young girl who still made up stories in an attempt to understand the world around her. Then there was the warrior who could push everything aside and do what needed to be done. And finally, there was the obedient slave who never questioned what she was told. The three sides seldom got along.

The one point of commonality was what she called *the sneak*—the aspect of Whisper that her mother had most prized. It had started with her chasing rabbits as a little girl. So long as she was running after them, they hopped away as if laughing at her. Only by approaching unseen and unheard could Whisper manage to pet their soft fur. From there, she progressed to the skittish coyotes and finally the falcons that hunted along the ridge. She'd only found playing the part of a slave tolerable because she knew she could escape at any moment.

She hopped from rock to boulder, remembering her time doing the same as a child and how that playfulness at avoiding detection had served her as an adult. Rule number one was to listen to her surroundings. Once she could identify the sources of the sounds, she could blend her movements into nature's music. Playing their parts in the day's concerto were the brushes on woodwinds, the growing storm to the south on percussion, and the cawing birds on horns. The scampering feet of small creatures rounded out the mountain orchestra.

She picked up human voices, like a discordant cough from the audience, beyond the next outcropping of rocks. The wind shifted slightly, bringing with it the smells of men, fire, and food. She hunched down behind a rock, as silent and invisible as a shadow.

"Her forces are weakened. Now's the time to strike," a husky masculine voice barked with authority. There was a loud strike of rock against rock.

"Because that strategy has worked so well in the past?" The higher squeaky voice reminded Whisper of an angry squirrel. A general murmuring of agreement was too indistinct for her to get a head count.

"Last's night's incursion proved we can get within their perimeter." Husky apparently wasn't giving up. "It's time we stopped raiding the outskirts of her base for supplies and take control. Sky can't hold out forever. She has to see that by now. One good attack, and we'll have her on the run."

"Or she's toying with us." The woman's words were punctuated by the sound of a stick against a rock. "Brigadier General Payne isn't like the last yahoos we had running that base. She's smart. You go balls to the wall against her, and she'll serve your dicks to her soldiers for lunch."

"So you think she's just been leaving the supply bunkers unprotected, available for us to raid like pet rats?" Squirrely Boy sounded nervous.

"I wouldn't call them unprotected," Husky said. From the sound of scratching in the dirt, Whisper imagined he was drawing a map of the compound. "If it weren't for our tunnel, we'd be facing a dozen tower-mounted machine guns. Whatever is inside the main camp is worth protecting. I say we send a small contingent in through the shaft. Then they take out the gunners. Without the guards watching, we can cut the fence. With a small enough force, we can take her before she knows what's happening."

"If we're going to go to all of that trouble," Squirrely said, "why not swoop in with our pickup trucks and load everything we find. Without provisions, she'll have to negotiate with us."

"I'm telling you," the woman said, "you're walking into a trap."

A stick snapped and was tossed into the fire with enough force to send sparks over the rock. "I'm in charge," Husky said. "We go in tonight. Everyone, get some rest."

Whisper stayed below the rocks and moved with the

wind toward a rustling manzanita bush. She needed to get a look at the dirt map before Husky kicked it to oblivion. If there was a tunnel into her mother's base, she might be able to sneak in before getting shot. Peeking over the edge of a large boulder, she got a good enough look at the raider's camp to get a head count and eye the stick-drawn lines in the ash-covered ground. There wasn't much to it—certainly no clearly marked entrance—but from the overlapping lines of sight from the guard towers, Whisper knew where to start looking.

ONCE THE BAND of thugs stopped wandering around, Whisper returned to her ascent of the mountain. Of the presented positions, she considered the woman's to be the most accurate. People had always underestimated Sky Payne, just as they had Whisper. She guessed it had something to do with their diminutive physical statures. There really wasn't much else the two women had in common.

The one thing Whisper was sure of was that her mother hadn't called her in to help with the fight. She hoped the woman at least expected Whisper's arrival. She couldn't imagine any other reason for sending out the coordinates except to call Whisper home.

The sun was climbing in the sky faster than Whisper was able to scale the ridge. Speed made for mistakes, but Roach was still down below in mortal danger. *Would it really be mortal if he's not fully human?*

She shook the foolish question from her head. Swash had made it clear he'd only wait until nightfall. Whisper needed to get into the camp before noon, get what she needed to help Roach, find her mother without getting shot, then convince the woman to help with the Beast. Though the base undoubtedly had a medical facility, she didn't dare betray Roach's situation until she knew what she was up against.

Her legs burned from the long night followed by the arduous climb. The idea of lying in her bunk, listening to long-forgotten music and fuming at pictures of Lindsey for being such a foolish girl, made Whisper want to cry. The Beast was as close to a home as any place she'd ever known. Even her early childhood hadn't been filled with as many people who truly cared about her.

As she came around a boulder that loomed over her, she caught sight of the army base with its evenly spaced round-roofed buildings, neatly organized lines of trucks, and soldiers moving with the precision of windup toys. She knew she'd found her mother's camp. The whirlybird that sat in the middle of the compound like some giant dragonfly confirmed that the brigadier general was in her lair.

Being situated in a natural bowl, the area was protected enough to support a grove of pine trees that ringed the base and stretched up to the ridgeline. It only took a couple of minutes with the binoculars for Whisper to spot the area of swept dirt. Footprints would have been a dead giveaway, but dirt scraped with branches worked almost as well. The woman raider was right. Brigadier General Sky Payne would have spotted the tunnel entrance on her first day running the base. She was playing with the raiders like a cat drawing in a mouse with a piece of cheese. As Whisper inspected the area, she considered the possibility that her mother had let the fools have their fun specifically to give Whisper a way into the camp.

She stashed her binoculars and scrambled back down the rock. Simply walking up to the front gate and announcing that she was the daughter of the woman in charge had its merits, most notably the saving of time. But Sky had warned Whisper not to reveal their connection, though she wouldn't explain why other than to say Whisper was on a secret mission.

I need her help, but I'll have to prove I'm worthy. Whisper resumed her nature-inspired movements along the rocks and trees. If anyone noticed her, they'd certainly raise an alarm. Being marched into camp at the end of a blaster would only earn her mother's wrath. And with the raiders making regular incursions onto the base, Brigadier General Payne would be all over her sentries to do a better job of protecting the camp. Everyone would be on heightened alert.

Sky might have her lookouts, but so did Whisper. Every living thing—the birds that squawked or took flight unexpectedly, the squirrels and other small scampering critters, the swarms of insects that moved like black clouds —told stories of where humans were lumbering. She pressed her back to a tree not fifty paces from the camp's wire fence. At her feet was a carpet of pine needles so dense the idiots might as well have laid out a welcome mat.

Beyond it were the scrape lines of recent use. After making sure her animal spies were comfortable with her presence, she bent down and slipped under the cover.

The husky leader of the raiders would have found the tunnel a snug fit, but Whisper had plenty of wiggle room. She wormed her way to the far end as silently as she could manage. Any good base security system would have ground-listening devices, something the raiders probably hadn't considered.

The tunnel ended at a ventilation duct rather than at a hole in the ground. She ran her fingers along the edge, wondering how the raiders could be so foolish as to think moving the sheet of metal wouldn't be heard by someone. She didn't have much choice but to use the same entrance. With one hand pressed against the thin sheet to keep it from rattling, she pulled on the screw that served as a handle. The hinged panel swung toward her. Opposite the entry into the metal shaft was a screen and, beyond that, a storage room.

You guys really had to work hard at pilfering supplies, didn't you? Fools.

She edged her way into the room and shut the access hatches. Being in the cook's pantry was a step forward, but it was still a long way from sneaking into the boss's office. The precious commodity of time was running out as fast as water out of a punctured bottle.

The comparison reminded her that she hadn't had anything to drink since leaving the cliff. Stitch's concoctions could have the effect of suppressing thirst and hunger in the interests of completing a mission, but that didn't alleviate the body's needs. She searched the shelves for something to drink. The gallon of rehydration fluid would be too big to haul back to Roach, but she managed to fill their water bottles without dumping the jug all over the floor. She drained hers in one gulp before refilling it.

At the door to the stairs, she flattened against the wall and listened. Above her, feet were scuffling—the short steps of a multilegged human millipede with each foot in an army boot. *Must be the lunch crowd.*

She eased the door open with her fingertips. A tight vibration made her stop. The hinge was dry enough to squeal on her if she pulled any farther. *You're running a sloppy organization, Mother. Or is this just another way to keep tabs on the raiders who've been sneaking in?* She reached for the jug of cooking oil at her feet and dosed the hinge. By the time someone noticed the mess, she'd be long gone. The door, properly lubricated, opened without a peep.

She crept up the wooden stairs to the metal door. A quick peek through the rounded window confirmed that the staff were finished with the equipment and tending to the serving portion of the meal. Masked by the noise of metal ladles hitting metal plates, she rushed through the industrial kitchen and out the back door.

Secure bases—be they military compounds, prisons, or slave pens—focused their sentries on the outside wall. What happened within the perimeter was usually far more casually observed. Even so, Whisper kept to the shadows and made only those sounds normal to the camp.

Two guards stood watch at an office door. From the flag overhead and the insignia on the fence post, Whisper knew she'd found her mother's base of operations. She hopped the fence then stood hidden next to the wall. Even when Whisper was a child, her mother had insisted on having meals with her men. The door squealed as it swung open. Three sets of footsteps hit the wooden steps with the precision of drumbeats. Leather against wood turned into leather against dirt just as the door's screeching returned.

Whisper darted out and flattened her body against the wooden porch before the last coil of the metal spring had its say. Her fingertips caught the closing door by the edge. Gently, she teased it back open just enough to slip through then silently guided the door back into its jamb.

WHISPER HATED WAITING—THERE was far too much to do— but it was the only way to ensure her mother's cooperation. At least, that was what she told herself repeatedly as she sat in the woman's office chair. The walls were covered with photographs of military personnel, impressive vehicles, and framed commendations. There wasn't a single visual mention of a family or personal life of any kind.

She wanted to slip her knife into the locks of the desk drawers, but she didn't see the point. There likely wasn't any information that would make life for Whisper any easier. She kicked her feet up onto the desk just as the screeching door to the receptionist's office announced the return of Brigadier General Sky Payne. Whisper forced her body to remain at ease as the office door swung open.

The woman with pressed army uniform, close-cropped hair, and commanding presence faced her and smiled. She let the door close behind her while eying Whisper. "Well done."

It was the highest compliment Whisper ever remembered receiving from her mother. "I'm hoping my incursion buys me more than your praise."

Sky took the visitor's chair instead of demanding her seat of power. "What do you need?"

Whisper lowered her feet and crossed her arms over the desk. "I didn't make it here on my own. I have a friend who's hurt out by the glass cliff and others stationed down below. We have a plan for getting them up here, but I need to know the area is secured before we try. I know you're dealing with raiders. They're planning an attack tonight."

Sky's squinty eyes and smile were almost as gratifying as the words of praise had been. "So that's how you got here? That nuclear-blast wall has been standing for decades— even before I was born. It's been considered unclimbable. I suppose it was my mistake for taking its impenetrability for granted just as my predecessors have done."

"So you'll help?" Whisper didn't have time for games.

"I'm sorry. I can't. If an attack is coming and I sent out a full contingent, I would be leaving the base exposed. As it is, the raiders control the land from the ridge to the wall."

Whisper wasn't surprised that her mother's first negotiating position was one of pigheadedness. "You called me here. You must have known that would have put me at great risk. Now that I'm in front of you, you're unwilling to pay the tab?"

Sky sat forward on her chair. "I'll have Shadow meet you at the camp gate. She can get you back to your friend without alerting the raiders. She's also very clever at detecting threats. After you two have left, I'll send a sortie toward the plain, away from your location. That should draw my enemies out from hiding. Once they make their attack, I'll be able to circle around from behind and trap them between my two forces. That should keep them more than occupied, but you still won't have long to retrieve your people. Those raiders are a slippery bunch. It's really the best I can do."

Whisper got to her feet. "When I return, we can talk about why you called me here."

Sky got up and extended her hand. "I look forward to it, daughter."

25

*a*t the army gate, a teenaged girl was tossing stones through the tight mesh at the soldier standing guard.

"Knock it off!" he yelled.

"Make me." She clocked him in the ribs. Her aim, from twenty feet away through the narrow openings, and was impressive.

"Why don't you run along home like a good little girl?"

"BGP called me." Another stone landed against the man's upturned arm.

"That's Brigadier General Payne to you," he said.

"*Pain* is correct. The rest is army bullshit."

Whisper cleared her throat to get the guard's attention. "I think she's waiting for me."

"You know this waif?" The man looked Whisper over. "Wait. Who are you?"

"A visitor. And I'm just leaving. If you have any

questions, I'm sure your commander can give you an explanation."

He unlocked the gate. "If it means getting rid of that brat, I'm happy to live with my confusion."

When Whisper exited the gate, the girl was already flitting through the woods like a camouflaged butterfly. She not only had Whisper's skills, but she knew the terrain as well. Whisper wasn't in the mood for another challenge. She raced through the forest after the girl without her usual care. Halfway up toward the ridge, she lost sight of her.

Sons of the rich. So far, the whole adventure to the camp had been a big disappointment. Roach was hurt. Swash was waiting impatiently. And Stitch and Blade would no doubt be debating what to do when the line didn't get thrown from the glass wall. *Screw it. I'm heading back to Roach. If Mother sends out her sortie, I can still signal Swash before nightfall. This annoying child can go play her games with someone else.*

Whisper catapulted off a boulder toward a flat rock. Halfway through the air, she felt arms wrap around her, sending her crashing into a bush of dense branches. From the ground, she looked into eyes so black she couldn't make out the pupils. The girl's black hair framed her face as she lifted her finger for silence.

The scuffle of running boots on dirt filled Whisper's ears. There were far more than the dozen commandoes she'd seen around the morning campfire. The girl kept Whisper pinned until well after the boots had passed by.

"Try to keep up this time." Shadow was off her and

shooting over the rocks before Whisper could get to her feet.

BACK AT THE WALL, Whisper pulled the rocks away from Roach's hideout. The sun was touching the horizon. They still had time, even if the desert floor was already in the shadows of dusk.

"How did it go?" His voice shook with pain and exhaustion.

She pulled the water bottle and tipped it to his lips. "We're okay for the time being. Mother is distracting the raiders from our location. She sent an annoying little girl to guide me back here and stand watch, but I lost her halfway down the mountain."

He turned away from the bottle and put his wrist to his mouth to suppress a cough. "It doesn't matter." He struggled out from under the rocks. "We need to tie the cable around that monster boulder then toss the line."

Whisper grabbed the shackled end. "I'll pull it around the rock. You get into position for the throw."

He nodded as he dragged the loop of line toward the edge. Based on Roach's labored breathing and limp leg, Whisper figured the Beast carrying Stitch and her medical equipment couldn't get up the cliff fast enough for him. Whisper walked backward toward the boulder as Roach paid out the line.

Halfway around, she found a freckle-faced blond girl

leaning against the rock with a smug look on her face. "I told you it was hard."

Whisper squeezed her eyes closed trying to reset whatever insanity had overtaken her. "Lindsey?" The long-dead girl had to be an illusion. Whisper shook her head, trying once again to see things clearly. "I don't know what game you're playing, Shadow, but it's not funny."

The girl stepped out from the rock and spread her arms. The skimpy bikini, copious amount of tanned skin, and far-too-well-water-plumped flesh could only exist in pictures. "You don't believe your eyes?"

Whisper pulled on the cable. "If you're not going to help, at least get your ghost ass out of the way. I don't have time for your shenanigans."

Lindsey moved just far enough away from the rock so that Whisper could pull the cable around it. "Whatever. I just wanted you to know I'm keeping watch."

"My guardian apparition—just what I've always wanted," Whisper said sarcastically. Insanity would have to wait.

She finished her circumference of the boulder and secured the shackle around the line.

With a quick nod, Roach heaved the cable clear of the cliff. "We need to get that Kevlar out and wrap it around the cable where it intersects the lip of the cliff. Even if the fabric shreds, it'll give the cable something other than the glass edge to roll against."

Whisper looked along the brush, wondering if Shadow was a mile away or right in front of her. "You didn't happen to see a girl sprinting among the rocks, did you?"

"There's no one here but you and me. You're probably hallucinating. Have you had anything to drink today?"

"I've been a little busy." She pulled her full bottle and took a long gulp. "How are you doing?"

"Apparently, better than you. Running around at this elevation without the proper hydration can make anyone a little loopy. All I had to do all day was keep to the shadows. Since I'm still conscious, the suit must be doing its job. Check over the side. If Swash saw our cable, the Beast should be rumbling out of its hiding spot. If not, we may be in trouble."

26

"I see the cable coming down, Captain."

Blade's announcement over the com set had Swash running for the bridge. The day spent doing chores while waiting impatiently for word from the away team made his skin crawl. Having Stitch pester him every five minutes to get some rest while he could only ensured that he kept as far from his bunk as possible.

He landed in the pilot seat and pulled the harness straps around his shoulders. "You'd better head for the jump spider. I'll open the protective shield then back the Beast up to the cliff so you can hook the line." Blast shields, plasma lance, hoists on both vehicles, titanium crampons, and every other detail of the operation had been checked and rechecked throughout the day.

"See you at the top of the cliff." The big man ran toward the back of the Beast like he was getting in position for an attack.

Through the view screen, Swash saw Stitch holding the plasma lance on the front catwalk. The long, ungainly power cord wound like a coiled serpent from the weapon-turned-drill to the battery under the rig. He smiled at her, remembering her nearly naked body pressed to his. Her return smile made him wonder if she was sharing the memory. *Probably not.*

He hit the starters to the Beast's twin multifuel engines. Their roar to life meant the end of a long day of waiting. Foot to accelerator, he rolled the rover out of its hiding spot. Metal plate after metal plate on the six wheels dug into the ground, pushed the vehicle up and forward, then crashed down with a crunch on the glass rocks, turning them to shards. With the wheel's protective armor in place, they wouldn't be setting any speed records.

Once fully on the scree, the rover moved a little easier. The rock pile shifted under the front tires, but at twenty-five tons, the Beast wasn't letting the rocks slide more than a few feet. The sounds of metal against metal and metal pulverizing rock were deafening. At the top of the pile, Swash swung the wheel, turning the bow away from the cliff. He could trust backing the rover only a couple of wheel plates, and even that needed to be over crushed rock. If one of the little sharp stones got under the overlapping armor, it could punch an impressive hole in the airless tire.

Blade's voice cracked over the headset. "Two feet to cliff face. One foot. Six inches. Stop, Captain. I can land the jump spider's wheels from here."

A light on the dash indicated Blade had released the security latch. Swash held the brakes, as if pressing harder to the pedal made any difference. From the back, clunking, whooshing, and finally an engine starting echoed up through the bridge's hatch. The back of the rover lifted slightly.

"I'm free, Captain."

"Thank you, Blade. Step one complete. I'm turning the Beast."

When he let his foot off the brake, the rover slid down the incline a few feet. Swash spun the steering wheel and gave the engines a little throttle. Though fifty feet long, fifteen feet wide, and twelve feet tall, the Beast pirouetted around on the loose rocks with the surefootedness of a cat. Stitch held onto the railing with one hand and the lance with the other. As Swash eased the Beast up to the vertical-hanging jump spider, Stitch guided the tip of the plasma lance into the open top and Blade's waiting hands.

The big man secured the barrel of the drill between the front seats. "Okay, here come the lines to your winches." He leaned under the seat.

Three ropes fell between the jump spider's rear wheels. Stitch took the belaying hook from the side of the catwalk and fished the loops of the three lines up to the permanently attached under-catwalk hoists. Blade tugged on each of the three lines tied off to the jump spider's upper roll bar then resumed his position behind the wheel. Without looking at the others, he hit the go-juice. The jump spider climbed the cliff like a toy insect. The modified winches at front and back of the sand rail spun a single loop each of the cable, holding the jump spider to the cliff but not rolling up the line.

Swash set the hand brake with all of the pull he could muster. As far as he was concerned, this was the scary part of the setup. He unhooked his harness. The rig was already at enough of an angle from the loose rocks that he had to keep his hand on the back wall for support. Opening the floor hatch in the middle of the bridge, he spotted the line trailing from the top of the cliff through the jump spider and ending just below him.

This is the kind of maneuver Roach would love. Too bad I don't have his flexibility. Swash knelt down then lowered his torso through the floor hatch. The spare winch, mounted to the frame like a giant bug, rested between the rungs of the short escape ladder. Swash fed the end of the cable through the winding hole in the drum then manually cranked it over enough times to be sure the line wouldn't fall out.

He reached for the sides of the hatch and pulled himself back into the bridge. His head was pounding from working at the strange angle. As he struggled to stand, the Beast slid another few feet down the slope. Swash snapped his head up to get a look out the front. The line up to the jump spider vibrated hard from the slippage, but both line and vehicle remained intact.

He struggled back to the driver's seat just as Stitch pulled herself into the navigator's chair. He looked at her over the open floor hatch. "You ready?"

"Would it matter if I said no?"

"Right." Some questions never really needed to be asked. Swash put the Beast in gear and released the brakes. "Okay, Blade. How are we looking?"

"That jerk of yours made my first drill hole a little

uneven, but the crampon feels tight. Let's hope Roach knew what he was talking about when he ran the numbers. I'm pulling the line from the winch now."

"Right." Swash doubted the slip would be the only mistake they made during the night. "Stitch, throw the lever to winch number one into slack mode." From under the catwalk, the metal cable followed the rope up and under the jump spider.

"Winch one connected to crampon," Blade said. "I'm moving the jump spider up to my next position. Good luck, Captain."

Swash nodded at Stitch then gave the Beast a taste of plant oil. When the front tires rubbed against the glass cliff, Stitch pulled on the lever to winch number one, engaging the electronic motor to retrieve the line.

The front of the giant rover pitched upward. All manner of disasters flashed in Swash's mind. *What if the engines can't operate when vertical? Will the metal plates really protect the tires or end up cracking the glass wall? Damn, that's a thin cord.*

"Hold," Blade yelled. "It's going to take a minute to get this second hole ready. Looks like this section of quartz might not contain as much metal. The lance isn't finding enough metal to lock onto. I need to reposition."

That's one I hadn't even thought of. Swash kept enough power to the tires to keep the Beast in position without pulling too hard on the line. "Roger. Let me know when you're ready." The military acknowledgement was a holdover from his time working under his grandfather. Swash knew the situation was dicey when he heard that word come out of his mouth.

Stitch kept her eyes on the cables. "Is this the craziest thing you've ever done with the Beast?"

He recognized her need for conversation during danger. "My grandfather used to drive this thing completely submerged. The dual snorkels can be extended ten feet over the roof. Scared the shit out of me the first time he did it. I was sure those flimsy breathing tubes were going to snap and drown us all."

"He sounds insane." Stitch played out the line of the second winch to Blade.

Swash let out a laugh. "He had no fear. That's for sure. My father was far more cautious. Craziest thing he ever did was trust people. We spent years transporting families to safer locations. At least, that was the plan. More than once, we ended up taking on people with not-so-honorable intentions."

"Okay, Captain," Blade said over the headset. "Give it a shot."

Swash gave the Beast a little accelerator before dialing up the torque. If the engines were going to quit, he didn't want them doing it while under heavy load. As the wheels began to turn, Stitch jockeyed the two winch levers. The temporary winding coil next to the ladder would take care of itself.

When Swash felt all of his weight transfer to the back of the pilot's seat, the three cables between the Beast and jump spider went tight. Even without air, freed from the vehicle's weight, the massive front wheels ballooned on either side of the cab. "Looks like we're off the ground. Status report."

The jump spider twisted from side to side. "The lance is

still working, though the underside of this buggy is getting a little warm. We probably shouldn't have completely removed the sand plate, but I think she'll be fine."

"Winches are holding." Stitch's voice vibrated as hard as the cables under the rig.

"Engines are humming." When it came to status, Swash felt the crew deserved to know the condition of his equipment as well. "One more pull, and I'll open the solar array. I don't want to risk it being at full flower until I know the panels won't get snagged on the rocks. Everyone, hang on." He gave the engines a solid shot of throttle. The time for pussyfooting around was over.

27

---

*a*fter twelve hours of drilling, pulling, and sweating, Swash had found his way around the constant state of terror. He'd never been a fan of heights, but as his grandfather would have said, tough noogies. The man had a way with words. By focusing on the rear of the jump spider, Swash could convince himself that they only needed to climb a little bit farther.

When Blade released his front winch and sailed the jump spider up and over the lip of the glass wall, Swash was faced with the wide-open sky of a new morning. "Just a little bit farther."

With the last of the crampons retrieved, Stitch secured the belt harness around her chest. "Would it be in bad taste to say it's all downhill from here?"

Swash struggled to contain his laugh. Between the stress, the sheer terror, and the lack of food and sleep, he feared that if he didn't control his reaction, he'd slip into full-on mania.

Blade stood on top of the wall and to the side of the Beast's nose with both thumbs up. "Roach found some good belaying boulders for the winch lines. Take it slow and easy. When those front tires clear the lip, there's going to be a sizable jolt. Not much we can do about that."

Swash nodded before realizing Blade might not be able to see him. "You did a fine job, Blade. I owe you a bottle of whiskey."

"Then you'd better not break it on the desert floor below."

Swash eased his foot down on the accelerator. "Everyone's a comedian."

When the huge front tires with their metal plates cleared the cliff wall, the pull from the winches caused the floor of the Beast to slam into the glass ledge, and the old girl shuddered from stem to stern. The lines went momentarily slack as Stitch struggled to draw in the cables fast enough to keep the vehicle from slipping down from its position. Glass shards shot through the open floor hatch. Swash's whole damn life felt like it was teetering on the edge of oblivion.

He reached for the individual wheel controls. By cutting the power to the front and rear wheels, he could focus all of the Beast's attention on the center two tires that were still in contact with the cliff, even if only barely. "Okay, Stitch. It's all you and me now. When you hear the engines roar, give those winches everything you've got. We need to get those center wheels up onto solid ground."

"I'm ready." Stitch's voice was still shaky from the climb.

Swash laid into the accelerator and held the useless wheel controlling the airborne tires with all of his strength. The rig rose a few inches then crashed back against the wall. The lines stretched out like the strings of a musical instrument, their groaning and twanging adding to the illusion.

He didn't have time to catch his breath. "One more time." He laid into the accelerator again. The sound of metal grinding against glass screeched through the open hatch. The rig climbed higher, but that only made the fall back against the glass more terrifying.

"You almost had it, Captain."

Though he appreciated Stitch's support, her encouragement didn't get them off the cliff any faster. He could tell the plan wasn't going to work. "We need to activate the temporary winch. I need the additional power and lower leverage point."

She looked at him with wide eyes. "How? I've got my hands full with the catwalk winches, and you can't leave the driver's seat."

"I've got you, boss." Roach's smiling face in the lower hatch made Swash wish he could bend down and kiss the kid.

"Be careful. This thing has been bouncing pretty hard off the lip. I'd hate to lose you, my friend."

"Now I know you're worn out," Roach said. "When you hear me yell, both of you give this monster everything she's got."

Swash looked forward out the view screen, terrified to see what might happen below the rig. "We're in your hands."

"Now!" Roach yelled. The bottom of the rig felt like someone was trying to pull it by the axles.

With every lever controlling the middle wheels already maxed out, Swash pushed the pedal to the floor. Stitch put her hands and forearms to the three winch levers and shoved them forward. Glass ground under the middle tires like cheese on a grater. The Beast lurched forward, then the front came down hard. Trees, bushes, and boulders flew at the front view screen as the rover's tires dug into the dirt. Crashing, bouncing, and rocking, the vehicle plowed over the open ground.

"You can let off the accelerator, boss," Roach said from under the rig.

Swash slid his foot to the side to get it off the pedal. As the vehicle slowed, he applied the brake handle until they were at a full stop. "Good going, crew. I couldn't be more proud of each one of you than I am at this moment—"

Bullets pummeled the view screen like locusts on a warm fall day, cutting short his victory speech.

"Fracking sons-of-the-rich raiders," Blade yelled over the com. "They must have waited until we did the hard work of getting the treasure chest up here before launching their attack." A lightning bolt erupted from his blaster, cutting short the barrage of pellets.

A girl's high-pitched battle cry echoed over Blade and Whisper's mics. Spears tipped with green-glass points sailed through the air toward the raiders. As the hidden contingent of children emerged from the shadows and engaged the raiders, Roach and Whisper climbed through the Beast's floor hatch.

"We need to get moving," Whisper said.

"Agreed." Swash put the Beast back in gear and hit the accelerator. The farther they could get from the cliff, the less likely someone would push them back over the edge. "Any hint on our support's strength?"

Whisper took over the navigator's chair from Stitch and launched the hummingbird drones. "It's a small group led by a child, but I don't think the attacking force is much bigger. Mother was supposed to be leading the main body of raiders away from our position. If all is going according to plan, she should have them pinned down at the base."

As the Beast powered past Blade, he swung onto the front catwalk. With blaster in hand and in the commanding position, he picked off raiders like he was swatting flies. "Apparently, they left a guard force behind," he yelled between plasma shots.

The hologram lit up the center console. "Where to, navigator?" Swash asked. He didn't like scrambling around in the middle of a firefight, especially after having just risked everyone's necks climbing the glass cliff.

"It took me half a day to climb up to my mother's base. If we go barreling in with these gas frackers on our tail, it'll just reinforce her enemy. All I'm seeing from the drones are rocks and shrubs."

A girl younger than Whisper swung down from a tree limb onto the catwalk opposite Blade. With a glare into the view screen, she aimed her hand toward a gap in the rocks then was off the rig and back into the battle like a bird who'd only momentarily lighted on the railing.

"That was Shadow," Whisper said. "Wherever she's guiding us is so well covered I can't make it out on the hologram. The drones aren't going to help. Do you want me to recall them or search for our own way out of here?"

Swash swung the Beast toward the gap. "Better bring our birds home now. If it is a hiding spot, we don't need to announce its location."

In the crumpled body suit, Roach looked like someone whose skin was falling off of his bones as he struggled into the observation chair. "I'm taking control of one of the drones. I can't leave the jump spider out there for the raiders to capture. Our sand rail doesn't have full remote control capabilities yet, but the servos are all installed. If I crash the hummingbird into the under-dash console, I should be able to maneuver it side-to-side against the levers. I can save her."

Swash never understood the technical aspects of what the kid created, and he had worries of his own driving the Beast. "Do what you have to do to."

The Beast climbed the short hill before any of the opposing force could break through the onslaught. Once through the gap, Swash turned the steering wheel to avoid plowing into a boulder. He didn't see the sharp drop-off until the rover was already sliding down the slope. "Hang on. Looks like we're in for a rough landing."

Rocks and gravel cascaded down the hill under their tires, making steering or stopping impossible. As the Beast fell below the level of the tree limbs, the incline leveled out.

From the harsh slamming of the metal plates that covered the tires against the ground, it was clear they weren't rolling over dirt. When Swash finally got the Beast under control and activated the outside lights, they were inside a concrete bunker.

"Well, what do you know about that?"

SWASH STARED straight ahead into the dark blankness of the tunnel like he was looking death in the face. His hands were still gripping the wheel when he felt a pinch on his arm.

"That should help you relax, Captain." Stitch stood next to him with an empty hypodermic in her hand.

"I guess I mentally locked up there for a moment." He willed his hands open and pulled his arms to his body. "I'm fine. We're still in danger. I need to stay alert."

"This is Shadow's lair," Whisper said. "She wants us to lay low until the fighting stops. We can't risk the raiders getting hold of the Beast. She knows what she's doing. Once it's safe to head to my mother's base, she'll send word."

"I don't know your mother, and I'm not putting our fate in the hands of some little girl." He struggled to keep his words in line.

"Completely understandable, Captain." Blade bent down and folded Swash over his shoulder. "We'll keep an eye on things while you catch a quick nap."

The bridge was receding in Swash's vision. Everything depended on him remaining in control. As he reached out toward the open hatch to grasp the far-off steering wheel,

Stitch took his hand. "It's okay, Captain. We're safe for the moment. I'll lie with you to help keep the nightmares at bay. If anything comes up that needs your attention, I'll be right next to you with the stimulant hypodermic at the ready. You've been at it for forty-eight hours. As the medic, I'm ordering you to get some rest."

The small spots that swirled around his sight grew larger and darker. He felt his body roll onto his bunk. "Keep the brake on."

Roach patted Swash on the shoulder. "Don't worry, Captain. I'll stay at the controls until you get up."

"You did good, Captain," Whisper said from behind Roach. "Get some rest."

Rest wasn't something Swash ever *got*. The alien concept usually conquered his waking mind. "Such a stupid saying."

Stitch rolled next to him then pulled down the privacy shield. "She only meant you deserve a break."

Swash shook his head. "Tell her I'm sorry. I didn't mean to say that out loud. She isn't stupid." His words sounded muffled.

"She knows." Stitch rolled him away from her, wrapped her arm over his chest, and pressed her body fully against his.

FLAMES SHOT twenty feet over the top of the Beast as if the devil himself were rising up from hell. Swash's heart stopped cold before firing off at twice its normal pace.

They're all going to die. The thought and image were ones he'd encountered too many times to recount.

"That ash hat sent us straight into a firestorm." Nado wasn't wrong. The guy had been loyal and an astute judge of character—more than worthy of being second-in-command. Unfortunately, his conclusions usually came too late to be of much use.

"I'll deal with Scorch later." Swash gripped the wheel, wishing it were the trader's throat.

"The question is, how do we get out of this hell?" Hammer Manchester never questioned an order, even the one that had led to his death. "I can't fly the drones in a firestorm, and if we're not careful, with this rocky coastline, we could drive straight over a cliff."

Swash turned the wheel toward a forest completely engulfed in flames. As the rover slammed into the first tree, the trunk exploded in a firework of sparks and flaming splinters that covered the view screen. "I'm heading for higher ground. So long as I keep us moving into the wind, we should eventually cross into the region where the flames have passed."

"Or hit the hottest section of the inferno. Our tires will melt eventually. The Beast isn't indestructible." Again, Nado's observations were all too accurate, just as they were too late in coming.

Undulating ethereal ribbons of red, yellow, and white covered the view screens like wraiths attempting to break in. Swash couldn't tell what remained solid from what had been fully consumed. With the front of the Beast pointed upward, all he could do was hope there was some escape on the path ahead. "Battery readout."

Nado reached over Swash's head and repeatedly flipped a switch as if hoping for a better outcome. "Failing, Captain. They must be shorting out from the melted metal under our feet."

Something shook Swash so hard he had trouble remaining in the driver's seat. He hung on tightly to the wheel. If he could just power over the ridge, he might still save his doomed crew.

"Swash, wake up. You're having a nightmare." Stitch's voice cut through the barrage of flames like a bucket of cold water, but the words were instantly turned to steam by the heat.

"Everyone, hang on. I'm engaging the multifuel engines. They're our only hope of climbing out of this hell." Something stung his ass like he'd just sat on a hot ember. He stomped on the accelerator. *The flames must be burning their way through the floor.*

"Swash! Wake up!" Something slapped him across the face like a flaming tree branch that had busted through the view screen.

"It's about to get hairy. The flames are inside the cabin. Everyone, back to the crew quarters, dog the hatch shut, and strap into your seats. There's nothing you can do for me now. No one's dying under my command." He fully intended to drive the torn-open front of the Beast straight through the flames. Even if his flesh burned from his bones, so long as the ligaments held the wheel straight and the accelerator to the floor, his crew might survive.

"Enough!" Stitch's brown eyes blazed through the flames of his insanity. The firestorm died down, the raging reds that shot up all around him settling into the subtle browns of the woman's hair that fell from around her eyes and caressed his face.

"I could have saved them." He wasn't sure if he was pleading to return to the fight or seeking confirmation of his incompetence.

As she shook her head, her hair waved about his face as if wiping away his guilt. "Only in your dreams. Tell me what happened to them."

He struggled to leave the past and return his thoughts to the present. "It was the air scoops. I didn't think to shut them off. My people died of asphyxia from the lack of oxygen. Because I was alone in the front cabin with the hatch sealed and the view screen ripped away, I was able to get enough oxygen. I passed out just as the Beast barreled beyond the fire line. When I came to, the living quarters had become a morgue."

She lay on top of him and wrapped her arms around the back of his shoulders. "I need you here to save us."

28

"We've got company, boss." Roach's voice over the intercom to Swash's bunk helped clear his head.

"Guess it's time for work. Thanks for sharing my nap." He hoped his tone was casual enough to keep Stitch from worrying about what she'd witnessed.

"Is that what it's like every night?"

"Only the ones when you drug me." He reached over her and pulled up the sliding side of the drum.

"I'll keep that in mind. Though in my defense, you weren't responsive behind the wheel." She hopped out first then helped him down, as if he hadn't been using the berth since he was a kid.

"I'm fine. Don't you have some medical thing you need to attend to?"

"I do want to check on Roach. Now that he's gotten some fluid into him, I'm less worried about peeling away his outer suit. Those cuts were pretty deep, but from the tone of his voice, I'm guessing there's another disaster brewing." She took Swash's arm and leaned in close. "If you can spare him, though, I'd appreciate the support. He's nearly as obstinate about refusing treatment as you are."

Swash led the way toward the bridge. "I doubt he'd have intruded unless it was important, but as soon as things calm down, I'll have him check in with you."

"Thank you, Swash." She let him go and returned to her medical unit.

Swash stood in the hatch to the bridge, staring at the armed warriors with their rifles pointed at the rig and wondering what the hell he'd gotten his crew into this time. "That's some welcoming party."

"About that," Whisper said. The girl was still in the navigation chair where he'd left her. "My mission is for my mother, not the military. As far as those soldiers are concerned, we're just some rover that managed to climb the cliff."

"Then who were those kids that saved us from the raiders?" Being in the middle of conflicting forces without knowing the players felt like a good way for Swash to lose another crew.

"My mother never believed in putting all of her trust in one organization—even one she's supposedly in charge of. There's always some higher command that is willing to sacrifice a base for unforeseen reasons, and armies are known to overthrow their commanders. General Payne believes in having options to fall back on in case things go wrong. Shadow's guerilla force lives in the ridge caves. She doesn't bow down to my mother, but she's no fan of the raiders who forced her people off their land and into the caves. That's about all I got out of the girl before she rounded up her troops and disappeared into the mountains. If things go frack water with my mother and we can escape her base, we might find help higher up in the range. As for those guards, they showed up not long after our rescuers left."

Wonderful, Swash thought. "Then tell me something useful about your mother. Time to play that daughter card."

"She has all the motherly instincts of a salmon. You know, the extinct fish? They used to lay their eggs unfertilized. Some random male would come along and squirt sperm all over the place. All the baby fish would know of its parents was the location of its birth. Those fracking fish would struggle with every ounce of their being to return to where they were born to do the whole dance again. That's me and my mother."

"If that was supposed to be reassuring, it failed." He wasn't sure what else he'd expected, but after all they'd endured, he'd hoped for something better.

"All I meant was, she doesn't work on emotion. She called me. I answered. She agreed to send her secret force because you're my support network. Her tactics gave us room to maneuver away from the raiders. If she'd rushed in with her platoon, that just would have told the raiders we were valuable to her. So I'm guessing those guards out front are for our protection."

Blade stood out on the catwalk with blaster in hand. "I'd

feel a whole lot more welcome if they'd lower those shoulder cannons."

Decision time, Swash thought. "Whisper, I'm relying on you to read the situation. Based on their uniforms, I'm assuming these are your mother's troops, but that could be a deception. You get some itchy feeling that things aren't as they seem, tell Roach. Roach, I want you to stay at the helm. If things turn ugly out there, back us the hell out of here. We may have to take our chances with the raiders. Blade, lower your weapon. I'm heading out to the catwalk to talk to these gas frackers, and I don't need things to get sparky."

"Understood, Captain." Blade reholstered his blaster but kept his hand on the end.

Swash stepped out onto the catwalk opposite Blade. A contingent of six soldiers, each equipped with weapons capable of cutting the Beast in two, stood in formation in front of the vehicle. "Can I help you, boys?" Swash did his best to keep his tone as casual as his words.

"Brigadier General Payne sent us. I'm here to bring you to the base." The soldier directly in front of the rover stood so ramrod straight that Swash wondered if even the Beast could knock him down.

"Well, seeing as how we've come all this way, I suppose stopping now wouldn't make any sense. Lead on."

The soldier shouldered his weapon and walked toward the ladder up to the catwalk.

"Hold it there, bucko." Blade said. "The captain said we'd follow you. There was no mention of you coming aboard."

The man stopped at the bottom step. "So long as you're on our base, your vehicle is under our command."

Swash pulled out his blaster and set it on the railing. "I'm not turning over the Beast. You can lead, and we'll follow, or I will come alone, but under no circumstances are you taking my rover. If your boss doesn't like my terms, she can come here and tell me herself."

The soldier stepped back and talked quietly into his com. He nodded before turning his attention back to Swash. "There's a maintenance garage halfway down this shaft where we can protect you and your vehicle. Keep to your electric motors. We don't need to announce this cave to the raiders. I do need to stand on your catwalk to direct your driver. These caves are a labyrinth of misdirection."

Swash returned his weapon to its holster. "Just you. Not your men. Blade will stay out here on the catwalk with you." He turned back toward the bridge before the man climbed the ladder. Dealing with military personal always felt like a battle of wills.

"I've got an itchy feeling about this, boss." Roach brought up all of the Beast's forward sensors. Green lines lit up along the edges of the view screen, indicating they weren't in danger of ramming into something.

"That's just your claustrophobia talking. How are our batts?" Swash asked.

"Nearly drained. The support rails took most of the impact against the glass ledge, so the additional battery damage was minimal, but drilling all of those holes and shooting the plasma cannon took every amp we were able to generate. We've got plant oil and go-juice, but those aren't going to do us much good if this turns into a firefight."

The military dude pointed straight ahead with his weapon, as if any other direction was an option.

"Keep the multifuel engines warm, but creep along on battery power," Swash said. "I don't want this guy to think we're out of firepower."

"You think they're really taking us somewhere for our protection?" Roach set the motors to one-tenth power. They rolled down the corridor at the same pace as the marching soldiers.

Swash knew when he was being taken captive. "My read is they're as distrustful of us as we are of them. They want us somewhere we're not a threat."

Red lines flashed on the screen as the rover left the concrete walls and floor of the entrance for the rough-hewn rock cave. Lights lit side passageways, some of them filled with ammunition and attack vehicles and others nothing more than tunnels that snaked into the mountain.

"Somebody's been busy," Roach said.

Swash nodded. "From the looks of the tunneling marks, I'd guess the military has been using these caves for hundreds of years. I wonder if even these military punks know where all of the accesses lead. If things get bad, we may want to skirt into this area. Whisper, think you could fly a drone down one of these holes?"

"It would be a challenge to maneuver it, but if the Beast would fit down the shaft, I'm certain a little ball of technology wouldn't be a problem."

Swash hoped it wouldn't come down to making a run for it, but having options always beat being stuck. "Keep your eyes open for possibilities." Even without the flying drones, a map recording their passage lit up the center console.

Their guide aimed them down a connecting cave to the right then another to the left. Whisper dutifully marked each turn on the scrolling map.

"Think they're trying to confuse us down here in this maze?" Roach edged the rover toward the side of the passage to gain a little more headroom.

"I wouldn't be surprised. They seem to be doing all they can to make sure we know we're at their mercy."

The Beast clunked down a small slope before the military contingent came to a stop. Their guide directed them into the brightly lit side chamber. Though the caves were rough-hewn, the garage was lined with concrete. Roach turned off the electric motors. "I guess this is our stop."

Swash straightened up. "We may be here for a bit. Whisper, you're with me. It's time I met this mother of yours. Roach, see Stitch about those wounds. Blade—"

"I'm standing guard, Captain."

"Good man. Try not to blast anything."

29

*S*wash hadn't actually believed Whisper when she'd talked about a secret military outpost high in the mountains. He hadn't even tried to imagine what it might look like. As the guard led him and Whisper out of the caves, through the main vehicle-maintenance depot, and out to the center of camp, he felt a little like Alice after she'd fallen down the rabbit hole into a foreign world.

Flanked by her guards, Brigadier General Sky Payne marched out from her offices. Their stride was as crisp and tailored as their uniforms. She stopped an arm's length from Swash. "Captain Jones, your reputation precedes you. A single person climbing the blast wall would have been unheard of, but hauling a twenty-five-ton rover up the glass face is the kind of thing that inspires legends."

Swash wished he'd changed out of the dirt-and-sweat-covered leathers—not that he owned anything that would have felt presentable compared to the woman's impeccable uniform. "I couldn't see leaving it behind. But just so we're clear, I didn't lift it off the desert floor to hand it over to you."

"Of course not. Forgive my troops for their hypervigilance. Technically, any military-type vehicle on my base falls under my jurisdiction, just as every soul is my responsibility. By keeping your rover in the tunnels, we've skirted that rule."

Though he appreciated the overture, being on the base made his skin crawl. Hopefully, the sooner he got some answers, the sooner they'd be able to get away. "Why, exactly, have you summoned your daughter and the rest of us along with her?"

The general took a deep breath. "While waiting, I've had some time to consider the best approach to gaining your assistance. I had prepared a number of speeches, but instead of the long song and dance, showing you the situation might cut out a lot of the reconstituted shit."

A loud whine from the giant mechanical bird in the center of camp preceded the long blades' slow rotation. The itchy feeling on the back of Swash's neck felt like a dozen Sierra-fever-carrying mosquitoes. "You expect me to get in that thing?"

The general turned toward the helicopter. "After what you all achieved by climbing the blast wall, I doubt you're intimidated by much. If you'd prefer the long song and dance, though, we can do that instead."

She had a point. "Lead on," he said.

The woman walked with the upright posture of someone used to shouldering command. Wind from the blades ruffled her short black hair as if impudent enough to think the elements outranked her. At the side door, she was helped aboard and handed a flight helmet. The deafening roar of the jet engine and increasingly spinning blades made talking impractical. She waved once then disappeared toward the cockpit.

Swash stood next to the gaping hole and ushered Whisper onto the craft. The smell of high-octane fuel burned his eyes and nose. The engine noise hurt his ears, and the spinning blades that threatened decapitation had him bending low. *At least I won't be losing the whole crew this time.* He grabbed the handrail and swung aboard just as the skids lifted off the ground.

Even though he was wearing a helmet, the roar around him made it impossible to think, let alone talk. He stuck close to the open hatch to view the world below. The military compound sat in a depression along a natural ridge that reached up to the mountain's summit like a precarious staircase. As they passed over the peak, he spotted a fortified dome in the distance, but instead of a cannon sticking its muzzle out, a telescope was aimed at the heavens. Beyond the structure, a series of satellite dishes looked like bugs sunning their wings. To his surprise, the helicopter banked away from the old technology and deeper into the mountain range's rocky crags. He scanned the valleys for any signs of life. The higher they climbed, the more inhospitable the cliff faces were. He was reminded of staring out the Beast's view screen at the raging ocean and rock spirals eager to impale him.

A hand grasped his shoulder. "Captain, check out what's ahead," Whisper said, distracting him from death's siren call.

Looking through the helicopter's front window, he at first thought he was staring into some trick of the light. Between a gap in the mountains, the grays, browns, and blacks of rocks and cliff faces were cut by greens, yellows, and blues. "What is it?"

"I suspect it's where we're headed."

The helicopter bent its face down, angling the blades into a high-speed attack toward the opening. The scream of the engine desperate to suck in more oxygen from the thin air indicated the bird was at the upper limit of its range. It weaved between the escarpments.

"Everyone, take your seats and strap in." The words blasted over his headset. "This is going to be a rough landing."

Swash kept his grip on the handrails of the metal seat long after a thump indicated that they had landed. The military personnel were the first to unlatch. When Whisper started fumbling with her harness, Swash mustered the inner strength to release his own latches. "Any idea what your mother is up to?"

Whisper stood and held the overhead strap. "I'm sure we'll find out soon enough."

He got up then jumped down from the craft, followed closely by Whisper. From their landing site, the area of bright colors was hidden behind a wall of boulders.

The general was the last to jump down from the craft. She yanked off her helmet, tossed it onto the floor of the helicopter, and shook out her short hair. "I want you to see firsthand what we're trying to do here. To limit contamination, we'll have to remain on the valley rim. Follow me."

Swash headed off behind General Payne. Whatever trouble she was leading them into, he wanted to face it before Whisper. A rush of warm humid air brushed his face just before a sneezing attack made him double over.

"Breathe through your mouth," General Payne said. "The pollen can get pretty intense."

As he took her advice, his eyes continued to burn, but at least his nose no longer tried to explode off of his face. "Pollen?"

"Before genetically modified gender unification, plants used to reproduce the way people do—with male and female."

He blew out of his nose with all the force he could muster. "You're saying I just breathed in plant sperm?"

She shrugged. "More or less." She resumed her climb up the small path.

Whisper bolted past him. "You don't mean…" Her words stopped when she came to a halt next to her mother. "Holy crap."

Swash hurried the remaining distance to the rim of the canyon. In the valley below, fields of uniformly sized plants swayed in the breeze, sending up clouds of yellow. "I've never seen an agrofield that big before."

"That's because it isn't one." The general hopped onto a

rock. "Everything below us is genetically pure, no modifications at all. We used the seed bank for our original parent plants. This area used to be a lake. When the water dried up, the soil underneath was rich in nutrients and free of pesticides and herbicides. It's taken decades of growth, hand pollination, and composting to achieve what you see. This valley grows all of the food we need to survive."

"How do you hand pollinate hectares of crops?" Whisper asked.

"Only the first generation of plants was pollinated by hand." General Payne pulled a vial from her pocket. Inside was a small yellow drone. "Robotic bees. We've got close to a million of them in the valley below. We call the farm *the seed*. It's our most precious secret, one we had to keep even from you. Until now."

Swash put his foot against the rock the woman was standing on. "So, you're a revivalist? I'm sorry. I just don't believe humanity can go back to the good old days."

Sky Payne shook her head like she couldn't believe how dense he was. "Many believe there was an apocalyptic domino effect. Bad weather and the extinction of insects necessitated genetically modified food crops that could grow fast with minimal water and nutrients. The results were plants that couldn't sustain life. Adding photosynthesizers helped create an edible product, but humans aren't the only ones who need to eat. And as more animals die off, the worse the apocalypse is becoming."

"I could argue with you all day, but that still wouldn't explain what I'm doing here. I doubt you hauled us up here to show off."

"My crops are failing, which is why I called Whisper."

He shook his head in confusion. "What did you expect her to do about it?"

"I need information."

Whisper finally turned away from the brightly colored fields. "You think the satellites will have what you need?"

"I hope so."

"And if they don't?" Swash asked. "Even if the information up there is retrievable, it would still be a hundred years out of date."

"I have to believe that there are other valleys like this one. I need to talk to their farmers. If the problem is with the original seed stock, we all will have suffered the same conditions. It could also be location dependent. Maybe it has something to do with being this high in elevation. Only by comparing notes can I get a handle on what to do next."

Swash couldn't believe he'd risked everyone's necks and dragged the Beast up the side of a mountain on strings just to play messenger boy. "Sounds like a foolishness to me. You can't stop a rock from rolling downhill, and you can't stop species from dying out. Based on our challenges in finding you—someone who *wanted* to meet us—chasing all over the country for hidden fields that might not even exist seems like a great way of getting shot. Hell, I'm not even sure what you're asking of us."

"I need you to find the key master. He can establish satellite communication among the agrobases. The future of the planet, and not just humanity, might well depend on it."

30

Back at the Beast, the more Swash went into the details of what Sky Payne wanted, the more of an idiot he felt.

"And you believed her?" Blade might have left his post on the catwalk, but he kept his eyes fixed on the guards on the view screen.

"Does it matter?" Swash asked as much to himself as the others. "She's willing to pay, and we need repairs. Roach, what's your take on their supplies?"

Roach tapped his fingers on the worksheet of busted parts. "She's got everything we need and then some. It's like they intentionally maneuvered us into this garage filled with rover parts just to taunt me. Give me six weeks of unimpeded access to this supply depot, and I'll have the Beast looking like new."

Swash had figured as much. "Stitch, you've been awfully quiet since we landed in this cave."

"I watch over the health of this crew."

"That's not really an answer." Swash again got the sneaky feeling she was hiding something.

"I don't trust the general. It's nothing personal regarding Whisper, but I've been around enough military people to know not to fall into their traps. They always have another agenda lying just below the surface."

"So, what are you suggesting?" Roach asked. "We try to barrel out of here? Because we're hardly in a position for a firefight."

"She holds all of the cards," Blade said. "She offers us everything we need if we help her and obliteration if we try and escape."

Swash wished there were another answer, but so far, his crew had only confirmed his fears. "Whisper, she's your mother. If I accept her help to get our asses out of here then head for parts unknown, what are the risks?"

"That would depend on which way we ran." She brought up a map of the area. "North is New Mormon territory. The third regeneration of Joseph Smith is a real piece of work. He's got all of the crazy with none of the charisma. His interpretation of *The Book of Mormon* relies heavily on subjugation of women. I know—that's where Mother sold me."

"You'd think someone so misogynistic wouldn't play nice with a woman general," Stitch said.

Whisper grimaced. "It's a truce of convenience more than shared values. The bottom line is, if we're seeking sanctuary, those fanatics won't be welcoming us into their cult for fear of alienating the general." The territory to the north turned red.

"And heading back the way we came is out of the question," Roach said. "I'm not dropping the Beast off that cliff."

Whisper turned that area orange, indicating it was bad but not as bad as heading north. As she expanded the map, a large black gash appeared to cut through the mountains and desert. "We've already discussed the dangers of coming too close to the nuclear trench." That area also turned red.

"How is her reach to the east?" Blade asked.

"We'd have to cross the rest of the Rockies first." Whisper changed the map into a three-dimensional topographical display. "We're high up in the first range, but there's a lot of territory between here and the Great Pains. Mother may not control all of it, but you can bet she'll have spies all along the region. She'll have her eyes on us from the moment we leave this base."

"We could still play along," Blade said. "She'd never know. Clearly, the key master isn't in these mountains. A little song and dance about starting our search in the Great Pains should buy us enough goodwill to get us out of the mountains."

"Then what?" Stitch asked. "That area of dust tornadoes and chemical contamination makes the desert look like an oasis. Our air filters would be clogged solid in a week."

Swash raised his hand to stop the potential bickering. "This is my rig and my decision. We need parts. I suppose the job she's laid out lies between white knight and bounty hunter. I can live with that, especially if it means we all keep eating. I want you all in on the negotiations. No one gets to come back at me months from now for having failed to snatch something important, so make a list of what you need."

SWASH HATED BEING INSIDE BUILDINGS. Every one he'd endured felt too much like a prison. Outdoors, where he had room to think, escape, and breathe without the threat of being poisoned, would have been more conducive to negotiations. Not that he had much of a choice. But at least the general met with him and his crew without guards standing watch at the doors.

"You've thrown a lot at me over the last few hours. Now that my people can hear firsthand what you have in mind, let's start with the basics. What, exactly, do you expect from us? I'm going to need more than a fake-sounding title to find this key master. Whisper has already told me what she knows, but I haven't heard anything that might help me find him."

Sky Payne unrolled a map of the night sky that covered the table. "These are the man-made objects I found with my telescope on the ridge. You'll notice that there's a lot of space junk up there. I can't verify how much of it is really garbage and how much is meant to throw someone like me off the scent. My point is, the circled pieces of hardware are birds that have let out a tweet in the time I've run this base."

Swash remembered the giant concrete bunker with

extended scope and accompanying satellite dishes. "How does this help?"

She spread another map across an adjoining table. "This is North America."

Whisper was all over the map like a kid turning a present in her hands and looking for the easiest way into the box. "All of my maps combined aren't half as detailed as this."

Sky Payne smiled. "That's one of the advantages of having a useable satellite."

Whisper jerked her head up. "I want access to our family's bird. That's my requirement."

Swash wasn't ready to begin negotiations, but the advantages of the girl's request were too obvious to ignore. "It would go a long way in helping us find this person you're after."

The woman shook her head. "It would be too dangerous. The only reason I downloaded information straight to the Beast was because I knew no one was watching. Without my eyes and ears up on that ridge, you'd be painting a big target on the top of your vehicle simply by turning on the bird."

This is why you don't start negotiations until all of your opponent's cards are on the table, he thought. However, Swash wasn't about to chastise a member of his crew in front of the competition. "So tell us what we're looking at."

General Payne returned her attention to the map. "As I was saying, lighting up one of the birds also highlights where the signal originated. I've mapped out every telecom land-based station with its corresponding satellite."

Even Swash could tell the numbers weren't adding up. "Looks like about half as many locations as satellites."

"That's about right. My guess is there's a rogue satellite up there that is firing up its companions. One of these land-based camps owns that rogue bird."

"The key master," Whisper said.

General Payne stood straight. "That's my hope."

Blade pointed a finger at the various bases. "There must be thirty satellite-listening installations on that map."

"Forty-seven to be exact, and I'm not positive that I have them all. I'm giving you a starting point."

"And what are you putting into the plan?" Blade asked. "I'm not doing battle with forty-seven armies just for the practice."

"I can't give you access to my satellite, but I can follow you. GPS might be dead, but that doesn't mean the trackers aren't still in every vehicle that wanders the earth. That's how I knew where to send the coordinates to Whisper. As each of these camps has a space bird, my bird can talk to theirs. When you're approaching a camp, I'll send you information on how to get in and access its satellite's controls. You won't be able to do much, but you should be able to ping my bird so I'll know you've found their satellite. I'll then return the ping. If other satellites echo the message, I'll know you've found our target."

"Right." Blade sounded completely unconvinced. "I'm just going to walk directly into the hands of a potential enemy, and you're magically going to make them lower their weapons. Then we waltz into their most secure location just to say hi to your bird." He turned to Swash. "Sorry, Captain. I'm out."

"Wait," Sky said. "Think of it this way. I'm giving you a list of supply depots and the keys to break in. I never said it would be easy, but that has to beat how you're scoring provisions currently."

Much as Swash didn't like it, she had a point. The opposite side of the coin—that she would be forever watching them—wasn't lost on him. If they decided to jackrabbit on her, she'd know about it. "Your plan seems long on desires but short on specifics."

"It beats being sent in as a slave," Whisper muttered barely loud enough to be heard.

"Fine." Sky straightened up from the map. "I'm willing to supply you with parts for your rover and a garage for you to work in, and I'll even stock your pantry so full you could eat like royalty. Just give me a list of what you want, and I'll make it happen. That should at least buy me access to half a dozen satellites. I don't care how you manage it. Don't use the bases if you don't want to, but I'll be expecting a ping on my satellite from six of these space birds on the map. How you manage it is your business."

Swash consulted the map. The ridges along the mountain range were littered with bases, but getting to them would involve a lot of climbing. South would be an option if they could figure out how to get past the nuclear trench. "And if I refuse?"

She waved toward the vehicle depot and the cave at the back. "Then you're free to leave. I won't stop you. Double-cross me, though, and you won't find a hole to hide in between here and the Atlantic Ocean."

Swash didn't need to look up to know every member of his team was staring at him. The Beast would need work just to get out of the cave. Medical supplies were barely more than hopes and prayers. The two plasma cannons had performed well, but their limitations were obvious. Going up against armies carrying projectile weapons would be suicide. Besides, Whisper hadn't forced them all this way just to have Swash chicken out at the last minute.

"You're not leaving me many options."

"I'm desperate, and you're my only hope. If you decide you want to use the bases, I'll do what I can to smooth the way. If connecting me to the satellites ends up being too difficult, I'd settle for communicating with other farms, though I wouldn't even know how to advise you on their locations."

In spite of the woman's commanding presence, Swash could hear the anxiety in her voice. "If you're unwilling to let Whisper access your satellite, how would we communicate?" Radio waves were only good until the next electromagnetic storm, and there was always something brewing on the horizon.

Whisper set a paper clip on the map. "If the satellite is always watching us, we can use that in our favor. I'd put a message on the roof of the Beast. We would just have to time it for when the sky is clear."

Swash rubbed the stubble on his chin. "So long as no one was above us, that would seem secure."

General Payne nodded. "I can't fire up my bird anytime I

want, but I should be able to contact you within twenty-four hours of seeing your signal." She stood up from her map. "So we have a deal, then?"

Swash felt like the walls were closing in on him. "Sounds like neither of us has much of a choice."

31

Swash stood at the entrance of the machine shop and gazed at the approaching night as the sun set over his shoulder. Six weeks in the compound had been a welcome break from the constant bombardment of life's struggles.

Roach closed up the jam-packed tool kit. "The Beast is repaired, fueled, and stocked to the roof, boss. I've been over every system twice, trying to come up with anything more I could wrangle out of their machine shop." In his crisp agroleathers, the pilot-mechanic cut a dashing figure. They were much better than the torn and stained overalls he usually wore.

Swash pointed at a rock outcropping just beyond the camp. "Round up the others and meet me on the ridge. I need to clear my head."

Roach patted him on the back. "You've got it, boss."

Though they were still outsiders as far as the base

personnel were concerned, the story of how they'd climbed the blast cliff had bought them a measure of begrudging admiration from the soldiers. Each gave Swash a crisp nod of acknowledgement as he passed. At the gate, the guard didn't even ask what business he had outside of the protective perimeter.

His new flex-sole boots conformed to the jagged rocks, making each step feel as surefooted as if Swash was climbing a set of stairs. The long cape hid the arsenal of weapons—both plasma based and projectile—from anyone who might be spying from the shadows. He almost wished someone would confront him just so he could try out the new blaster. With the equipment the general had foisted on him, he felt downright invincible.

At the crest of the ridge, he stared out at the mountain range. Though the brigadier general's helicopter was impressive, it wouldn't be able to lift the Beast over the passes. Swash and crew were in for a long hard slog over and down the mountains. There wasn't much to be done about it, though. It wasn't like he wanted to head back the way they'd come.

"We're all here, Captain." Blade's husky voice behind Swash cut through his contemplation.

He turned to face his crew. "None of you signed on to risk your lives in pursuit of some half-baked scheme to save the planet. As for me, I don't like being a pawn in someone else's game, but my word does mean something. I know the rig is loaded, and from your shiny new duds, I can see you've been as seduced as I have by the general's bounty. However, each of you can still turn away. Her agreement is with me. She'll be watching the Beast, not worrying about a bunch of individuals who've thought better of their captain's harebrained scheme. All I ask is that you be honest with me." He locked eyes with Whisper, figuring she'd be the most adamant in her opinion.

The girl put her hands in the back pockets of her formfitting body suit and looked down at her boots. "My mother can be very persuasive when she wants to be. I've been a spy in her cause for as long as I can remember. It's my fault you're all up here." She turned her eyes back to Swash. "You're the only real family I've known. I didn't even understand the term until you took me in. If we go in search of the key master, I'll be forever worried about what I've gotten you all into, but at least I'll be there to help. If any of you decide not to take up my mother's mission, she might insist on using me as bait to find another champion. We climbed the blast wall as a team, and that's what she's hiring. Either way, I'm screwed."

Swash would have liked to let the girl off the hook and tell her she'd always have a home on the Beast and that nothing that had happened or would happen was her fault. He wanted to say something encouraging, but he also didn't want to lie to her. Sky Payne was a powerful woman. If she decided Whisper was to return to her service, Swash doubted there was much he could do about it.

Roach rescued Swash from his discomfort. "I'm with you, boss, no matter the adventure. Using General Payne's information, we'd at least be hopscotching between resupply depots. That's gotta count for something. I don't for a minute believe that creating utopian farms is going to change anything, but that's not my problem. Keeping the Beast functional is. It's not like she's telling us to change our ways. All she's asking is for a say in our direction."

Swash nodded and smiled. Roach always was the practical thinker. He moved his stare over to Blade.

The weapons master rested his hands on the minicannons strapped to his sides. "However far her military influence stretches, having her on our side sure beats fighting against her. There's a lot of bad land out there. If we're not going to settle down somewhere, I'd just as soon have the help."

"It doesn't worry you that she's sending us into what are probably the most dangerous areas?" Swash asked.

Blade looked out the way Swash had been gazing when he'd climbed the ridge. "We've done remarkably well up to this point—far better than I expected. If everything goes frack water on us, we can always change our minds. In spite of her threats of retaliation, I've never run across any form of law in my travels that extended beyond a post's perimeter. She might have control of that little hole in the ground, but the raiders are proof enough that she can't enforce her will far from home. I have to believe the farther we get from this mountain, the less influence she carries. I say we take her up on her offer until it's no longer convenient. Then we do what's best for us. No one can expect more."

"What are your thoughts?" Swash asked Stitch. As always, he felt like he was prying the answer out of her.

"I don't like being beholden to others."

Her answer surprised him. "I would have thought you'd be all over the idea of fixing the apocalypse."

Stitch shook her head. "Like Roach, I don't think it'll work. Her struggling farm seems like a nice, pretty way of getting us to find this key master. Turning the satellites back on seems like a bad idea to me."

Swash found a nearby rock and took a seat. Of all of them, Stitch was the most thoughtful. If she had concerns, he wanted to hear and understand each one. "You don't think it's a good idea for people to communicate?"

"People, yes, but we're talking Tower of Babel stuff here."

Her thoughts left his thinking in the dust. "Explain."

She waved her arms at the sky as if addressing all of humanity. "We thought we were so smart. Man could rival God. If only we could share information, then there would be no limits on what we could achieve. But we were wrong. So very, very wrong. People are a contentious, duplicitous, greedy species." She looked around at each member of the crew. "Something changes when people are physically together, sharing hardships. Like Whisper said, we're family. That connection isn't possible if all we see of each other is what's on a view screen."

Blade fondled his weapons. "You make it sound like the wars were a good thing."

"I think they were inevitable," Stitch said. "Not that it matters. They're history now. It's like we're constantly saying—we can't go back, only forward."

Swash didn't want to lose Stitch, but so far, she was the only one balking at the mission. "And if we follow the general's plan in spite of your misgivings?"

"At the risk of sounding like Blade, I'll go along until I no longer find it feasible to do so. My take on things is that, ultimately, you're going to have to throw in with the general or rebel against her. What happens when you do find this key master? From his attempted secrecy, I have to believe he's not going to deal with her without a fight. Are you going to be her strong arm?"

Swash hadn't considered having to play the goon. "There's a lot of land, gangs, and environmental dangers between here and there. The likelihood is we never find him. Blade, what do you put our odds at?"

"Assuming we don't die at the hands of marauders first, a hundred to one that we make it to the first outpost. A thousand to one that we make it to all six. As for finding one individual on a continent of twelve million? Well, that kind of answers itself. I've had a look at the general's map of bases. She's not doing us any favors in where she's sending us."

Whisper took Stitch's hand. "If we're the ones to find the key master, we'll have a say in what happens. We don't have to turn him over to my mother if he can present a stronger argument against it."

"And if he's actually trying to rebuild the network on his own?" Stitch asked. "From what I've heard, we may be stepping into the middle of another war, and I'd just as soon not be remembered as the catalyst that ended humanity's last breath."

"If we all die, who's left to remember?" Blade asked.

Swash could feel decision time creeping up on him like a bad cold. "I have no intention of emptying the Beast's storage lockers, so whether it's a lie or the truth, either way, we're leaving with a full rig. So long as you're all with me, I don't see any harm in agreeing with the general's request—for now, at least." He watched Whisper for her reaction to the potential theft.

"That's good enough for me to convince my mother to let me remain on board," she said. "So long as you can live with the potential of me being a spy for her."

"I'll take that chance."

BOOK LIST

Technopia Series:
(writing as Greg Chase)
Creation
Evolution
Damnation
Salvation

The Malveaux Curse Mysteries :
(writing as G.A. Chase)
Dog Days of Voodoo
You, Me, and the Voodoo Queen
Oops! I Voodooed Again
Voodoo You Love
Voodoo You Think You Are
Look What You Made Me Voodoo
Love Me Like Voodoo

The Devil's Daughter:
(writing as G.A. Chase)
Hell in a Head Gasket
Hell Bent for Demons
Hell's Highway

Hell or High Water
Hell Away from Home
Hell and Back

<u>Driving Force:</u>
(writing as Greg Chase)
The Road from Oblivion
The Road Forsaken
The Road to Survival

ABOUT THE AUTHOR

Greg Chase is a science fiction and paranormal author living in New Orleans with his wife, fellow author Deanna Chase, and their two shih tzu dogs. On any given day you can find him behind his computer, people watching in the Quarter, or out in his studio creating stories in glass. His glass work can be found at www.chase-designs.com.

gregchaseauthor.com